For more than forty years,
Yearling has been the leading name
in classic and award-winning literature
for young readers.

Yearling books feature children's
favorite authors and characters,
providing dynamic stories of adventure,
humor, history, mystery, and fantasy.

Trust Yearling paperbacks to entertain,
inspire, and promote the love of reading
in all children.

OTHER YEARLING BOOKS YOU WILL ENJOY

by Thomas E. Sniegoski

illustrated by Eric Powell

A YEARLING BOOK

Text copyright © 2007 by Thomas E. Sniegoski
Illustrations copyright © 2007 by Eric Powell

Visit us on the Web! www.randomhouse.com/kids

Educators and librarians, for a variety of teaching tools, visit us at
www.randomhouse.com/teachers

ISBN: 978-0-440-42180-1 (Trade)
ISBN: 978-0-385-90402-5 (GLB)

Printed in the United States of America

July 2007

10 9 8 7 6 5 4 3 2 1

For Gerald W. Cole. I think you would've really liked this Hooten kid.

ACKNOWLEDGMENTS

As always, much love and thanks to LeeAnne and Mulder for putting up with my nonsense.

Special gold-plated thanks go out to Stephanie Lane for not calling the men in the white coats when she read this proposal, and to Liesa Abrams for introducing us.

Thanks also are due to Christopher Golden, Dave "I don't like it" Kraus, Eric "You want me to draw what?" Powell, John & Jana, Harry & Hugo, Don Kramer, Greg Skopis, Mom & Dad Sniegoski, David Carroll, Ken Curtis, Mom & Dad Fogg, Lisa Clancy, Zach Howard, Kim & Abby, Jon & Flo, Pat & Bob, Pete Donaldson, Jay Sanders, Timothy Cole and the Flock of Fury down at Cole's Comics in the city of sin.

This one is for the crazy kid inside all of us.

CHAPTER 1

Billy Hooten was weird.

At least, that was what everybody said.

He had always loved things strange and unusual. Halloween was his favorite holiday; he liked it even more than Christmas. He loved building things like robots, although they very rarely worked, and monster movies, especially old ones, and comic books, but even better was drawing his very own monster comic book. If all that made him weird, then Billy supposed people were right.

On a cool Saturday morning in September, Billy was doing one of those things he loved most—sitting on the old stone wall that separated his backyard from the

Pine Hill Cemetery, reading the latest issue of *Snake*. He'd picked it up from the Hero's Hovel Comic Book Shop on his way home from school the previous day. It was issue number 344, featuring the Snake's most evil nemesis, the Mongoose.

He was getting close to the end of the comic, which he always hated because it meant waiting another whole month for the Snake's next adventure. He held his breath as he slowly turned to the last page. The Mongoose had captured the Snake and chained him to a missile, ready to shoot the hero out into space.

And then Billy read a comic book fan's most dreaded words—TO BE CONTINUED!

He groaned aloud and put the comic down, trying to relax. It would be a month before the next issue of *Snake* was available. *A month isn't so bad*, he tried to convince himself. It was only four weeks, and four weeks was only a little bit longer than three. He was pretty sure he could make it, but just in case, he decided he'd reread all the old issues in his *Snake* collection. By the time he was finished, he figured issue number 345 would be just about ready to hit the shelves.

Billy immediately felt calmer and was about to head back inside to his room when he caught a movement out of the corner of his eye. From his perch atop the wall, he looked out over the sea of headstones and crypts that had been a part of his life since his family moved to this house on Pine Hill nine years ago. Most of the other kids thought the cemetery was creepy, but twelve-year-old Billy had never had a problem with it. Sure, it could be kinda scary when it was really dark and the moon was full, but he liked that sort of thing.

Billy squinted. He thought the movement he'd seen might have been Tommy Stanley and his little brother, Stevie, from two streets over. The Stanley boys were mostly into wrestling, but they liked comic books, too. Billy certainly didn't find wrestling as cool as comics, but he had learned to be tolerant of other people's likes. He stood up on the wall and waved to the boys, wondering if they had read the latest issue of *Snake*.

"Hey, Hooten!" one of the boys called out.

The two figures were heading directly toward him, walking down one of the many footpaths that wound through the old cemetery.

"Whatcha doin' up there, making a nest?" asked the other.

The boys were close enough now that Billy could see them, and suddenly he realized that it wasn't the Stanley brothers at all. Indeed, these boys were much worse—Randy Kulkowski and his weaselly sidekick,

Mitchell Spivey. When these two were together, it spelled trouble with a capital *T*.

"Oh, crap," Billy muttered, his stomach doing backflips that would have made the midget acrobats he had seen at the circus last year green with envy.

"Hoo! Hoo! Hoo!" Randy called out as Mitchell cackled beside him. "I'm talking to you, Owlboy," he taunted. "Why ain't you answering me?"

Billy laughed nervously. "That's pretty funny, Randy. Can't get enough of those Owlboy jokes."

Billy had hated Randy Kulkowski for as long as he could remember. He hated everything about him, from the top of his gigantic square head to the tips of his clown-sized feet. Randy was to Billy what the Mongoose was to the Snake, and the two had been in every grade together since their first day of kindergarten. Billy remembered his first encounter with Randy. It had involved a medieval battleaxe made out of LEGOs. He reached up and rubbed his scalp, certain he could still feel the bump there. He often wondered what horrible thing he might have done in a previous life to be cursed with the likes of Randy Kulkowski.

Randy and Mitchell left the path and clomped across the recently mowed grass. They carried baseball bats slung over their shoulders, looking like cavemen out hunting for food. He guessed that Randy and Mitchell would have been pretty comfortable living in caveman times. Too bad they hadn't, because that meant they were here to bother him now.

"We were going over to Berry Park to hit some balls, and I said to Mitch here, 'Hey, look, there's my good friend Billy Hooten waving to us, maybe he'd like to come along,' isn't that right, Mitchell?" Randy asked, a grin that gave Billy the urge to pee spreading across his extra-wide caveman face.

Mitchell giggled like a crazy person, running the back of his hand across his constantly runny nose. "Yeah, man," he answered in his high-pitched voice. "You said, 'Hey, there's Hooten the Owlboy, let's get him to play ball with us.' "

Hooten the Owlboy. Randy had come up with that nickname way back in kindergarten. He'd said Billy's round glasses and last name reminded him of an owl. So Owlboy Billy had become. Billy didn't particularly care for the nickname, especially when Randy used it around the other kids at school. But he guessed it could have been worse.

"So what do you think?" Randy asked with a twisted grin, striking the palm of his hand repeatedly with the baseball bat. "You comin' or not?"

There was no way Billy was going anywhere with

Randy and Mitchell. Baseballs wouldn't be the only things hit with those bats.

"Geez, Randy," Billy began, his mind quickly scrolling through his list of foolproof excuses. "I'd love to, but . . ."

Sorry, I have to take a bath. (Not late enough in the day for that one.)

I have to go with my parents to visit my aunt in the hospital who just had both lungs taken out. (Too dramatic.)

I have a really bad case of diarrhea. (Nope. That one might result in his nickname being changed to something really clever like Poopboy or Captain Craptastic.)

I have to stick around and do my chores. (Bingo! Who could argue with chores? They were a sad fact of life for every kid.)

". . . I've got to stick around here and do my chores." Billy shrugged and shook his head, doing his best to look disappointed. "I woulda liked to, really, but—"

Billy was interrupted by the squeak of the back door opening. He turned to see his mother coming out of the house.

"Billy, honey, who are you talking to?" she called. She had her purse slung over her arm and her car keys out.

"*Honey,*" Mitchell mocked in a low voice. He giggled evilly.

"Um, just some . . . friends."

His mother walked across the lawn to Billy and stood on her tiptoes to look over the wall at the grinning faces of Randy and Mitchell.

"Oh, hello, boys," she said. "What's going on?"

"Baseball," Randy grunted, showing her his bat and dangling glove.

A huge smile spread across Mrs. Hooten's face as she turned to Billy. "Baseball? You're going to play *baseball?*"

His mother always got excited when she thought he was about to do something she considered normal. She and his dad weren't too crazy about the stuff Billy liked: comic books, monster movies, robots. They were constantly telling him that those things would give him brain damage and trying to trick him into doing stuff "regular" kids did. Like baseball.

"I would've loved to," he explained. "But as I was saying, my chores are going to pretty much keep me tied up for the day."

"Chores shmores!" his mother said, throwing her hands in the air. "You just go off and have a good time playing with your friends. We'll worry about chores later, how's that?"

Billy's "friends" smirked at him like a pair of sharks at an all-you-can-eat people buffet.

He had to think fast.

"Okay," he said, pretending he was about to jump down off the wall to the cemetery side. "I just hope Dad doesn't get mad."

"Why would Dad get mad?" his mother asked, a puzzled frown on her face.

Mrs. Hooten had a really bad memory, and Billy was hoping he could put that to good use now. "Remember he wanted the garage cleaned so he could get to the snowblower?"

His father hated to shovel and swore after every snowstorm that he was going to buy the biggest snowblower he could find.

"Snowblower?" his mother asked, a look of real confusion on her face now. She glanced up into the September sky as if searching for the first drifting flakes. "But we don't have a snowblower . . . do we?"

"No," Billy said. "But we should. According to the *Farmer's Almanac*, we're in for one bad winter, as much as a hundred feet of snow."

"Oh my," his mother gasped. "We really should buy a snowblower!"

"That's a great idea," Billy said. "But where could we keep it?" He rubbed his chin, pretending to be deep in thought. "There's always the garage, but that's such a mess. . . ."

"Then we'll just have to clean it," his mother said

firmly, obviously having made up her mind. "Today. Who knows when the first storm will hit?" She turned her nervous gaze to the perfectly clear fall sky.

"So that means I can't play ball with my friends?" Billy asked, allowing just the right amount of disappointment into his voice.

"I'm sorry, honey," Mrs. Hooten said apologetically, reaching out to pat his knee. "But there'll be no baseball until that garage is cleaned."

"But Mom . . . ," Billy began to protest, giving the performance of a lifetime.

"No, I've made up my mind, Billy," she told him. "I'm sure your friends understand."

Billy tried to look sad as he spoke to the two creeps below him. "Sorry, guys," he said, shrugging. "I tried, but chores come first. Maybe some other time."

Like when the two of you learn to walk and chew gum at the same time, Billy thought as he watched Randy and Mitchell wander away, already losing interest in him. He breathed a sigh of relief.

"They seem like nice boys," his mom said.

"I guess," Billy replied.

"Don't worry, honey." She reached out and squeezed his hand. "I'm sure there'll be plenty of other opportunities to play with your friends."

"Oh, joy," Billy said sarcastically, trying to formulate

a plan that would allow him to avoid Randy for the rest of his life. The only one he could think of involved moving to Antarctica.

Billy's mother began to rummage through her purse. He guessed she was looking for her car keys and reminded her that she was still holding them in her hand.

"I swear I'd lose my head if it wasn't attached," she said with a laugh, moving away from the wall and toward the driveway.

Billy pictured all the places his mother could leave her head. It would probably be a full-time job to keep an eye on her noggin. He grabbed his comic book and hopped down off the wall, following her toward the car.

She stopped and turned to him. "What were we talking about again? I've completely lost my train of thought."

This happened to his mother a lot. Not only did she lose the train, but frequently she lost the tracks as well. No matter, it meant he wouldn't have to clean the garage today after all.

"You were saying you had to run some errands," Billy offered.

"That's right," she said, pulling her shopping list from her purse. "I've got to go grocery shopping. Want to come?"

Billy had a hard time deciding which would be worse, hanging with Randy and Mitchell or going grocery shopping with his mother. The two were pretty much a tie in the most-horrible-way-to-spend-a-Saturday-afternoon category.

"No, that's all right," he answered. "I've got some things I have to do around here."

"I'm sure you do," she said with a smile, ruffling his sandy blond hair as she got into the car. "Keep out of trouble."

"I'll do my best," he called out as she carefully backed down the driveway and out onto the street.

She beeped the horn twice, and with a wave she was off.

Billy stood in the middle of the driveway for a few minutes thinking about all the things he could do with his day now that he was free from the clutches of Randy Kulkowski. He considered trying to fix the robot he'd built recently, but he wasn't sure if he had the parts. How about a freeze gun? *That might be cool*, he thought, remembering the broken air conditioner he'd recently found by the side of the road and hauled back to the garage on his wagon. He'd also come across some old fire extinguishers not too long ago, and thought about creating a jet pack. *So many inventions, so little time*, he mused.

He turned and walked toward the back porch. Before he did anything, he had to put away his comic book. All his *Snake* comics were in mint condition and he wanted them to stay that way.

He had one foot on the back steps when he heard the sound. At first he thought it was a squawking bird, maybe a noisy crow, but as he stopped to listen, he realized it wasn't that at all.

It was a voice, calling for help.

Billy placed his comic on a plastic chair on the porch and stepped back into the yard.

"*Help!*" cried the voice again, carried on the gentle breeze that ruffled Billy's hair. The cry was coming from somewhere inside Pine Hill Cemetery.

Billy considered running into the house to get his dad, but something told him that if he waited, it would be too late.

Too late for what? he wondered.

"*Oh, help me, please!*"

Without another thought, Billy climbed up onto the stone wall and jumped down into the cemetery, running as fast as he could toward the sound of the voice.

He ran into the oldest section of the cemetery and came to a screeching halt in front of a great stone mausoleum. But it wasn't just any mausoleum. It was the largest crypt in the entire cemetery and had been built by the Sprylock family over a hundred years ago. The Sprylocks were supposed to have been warlocks and witches, and their stone resting place was said to be haunted. Billy nearly jumped out of his skin when he heard the voice again. It was coming from inside the crypt.

"Somebody please help!"

The door of the crypt was slightly ajar, and for a moment Billy entertained the idea that Randy and Mitchell might be playing a trick on him. But then he heard another voice inside. This one was low and grumbling, like somebody with a bad cold and a lot of phlegm in his throat.

"Hold still, you little creep, so's I can crush you like the bug that you are!"

Billy grabbed hold of the thick, rusted metal door and pushed it open, charging into the crypt.

Then he stopped short. It was like a scene out of one of his comic books. The Sprylock family mausoleum was in total disarray, coffins broken, bones scattered everywhere. Standing in the middle of the room were two of the strangest-looking people he had ever seen in his life.

"It *is* you!" said the smaller of the pair as if he'd been expecting Billy all along.

He was short, really short, with beady little eyes, and he was dressed in a tuxedo. Huge pointy ears stuck out from the sides of an enormous head that reminded Billy of a summer squash.

"I'm saved!" the creepy character screeched with excitement.

Billy was confused. The little guy was talking as if he knew him, but Billy had never seen him before. He'd definitely remember a guy who looked like that.

"I'll crush *him*, too!" roared the other one, and Billy nearly fainted when he got a good look at him. This guy was built like a professional wrestler, with a huge upper body, great big arms, a teeny tiny waist and spindly little legs. And if that wasn't weird enough, he had the head of a pig. *No, not a pig, a boar . . . tusks and all!*

It was the scariest thing he had ever seen in his entire life—even scarier then Randy Kulkowski—and it was lumbering directly for him. Billy stood frozen; his eyes locked on its gross face, on the large brownish warts with little hairs sticking out of them, on the yellow, watery eyes, looking for some clue that the guy was just wearing a really cool mask, but from what he could tell, it was all real.

Billy didn't know what to do. His brain was sputtering like the old computer at the back of Mrs. Maloney's class that had to have been built when dinosaurs walked the earth.

"Wish I had some bread," the pig-man roared, his muscular, hairy arms reaching out for Billy. "Bet you'd make a really tasty sandwich."

That got Billy, and he did something he'd never have imagined doing in a thousand and one years. He reached down, snatching up what looked like a leg bone from the ground, and stood ready to defend himself against the advancing brute.

Billy had been in lots of fights in his twelve years. He'd never started any of them, and never won any of them, either. But this was different. This wasn't somebody knocking him down because his mother had made him wear that sweater with the dancing snowmen on it to school, or shoving his head in the toilet for an ultimate swirly because he had accidentally reminded the teacher about a homework assignment she'd forgotten to collect.

This was real, life-or-death stuff.

The monster was almost on him, his stink making Billy want to hurl.

Billy reared back with the bone, remembering what his dad had tried to teach him about hitting a baseball—to keep his eye on the ball, only in this case it was the pig.

What happened next was something Billy would never have believed if he'd read it in his comic books or seen it in his movies.

He was just about to swing the bone at the pig-man when the beast slipped on a pile of bones. A slip of

Olympic caliber, the kind of slip that if it had happened in the hallway at school would still be talked about five years later.

Remember when what's-his-name slipped that day?

Dude, that was totally outrageous! I thought for sure he was dead.

The pig-man's feet flew out from beneath him, and Billy could've sworn he heard that crazy whistling sound he always heard in the cartoons as the creature landed, the back of its big head whacking the mausoleum floor and making Billy wince.

He watched the beast for a moment, waiting for signs of movement. Nope, knocked out cold.

Talk about lucky.

Then the fact that Billy was holding something that had once been inside a human body suddenly began to sink in and he dropped the bone to the ground, wiping his hands furiously on his sweatshirt.

"I knew it," screeched the creepy little guy with the squash-shaped head.

Billy jumped. He'd nearly forgotten about the other creature.

"I knew I would find you if I came to the world above. I knew it!" The creature smiled, showing off a set of teeth that would have made Billy's dentist drool.

Billy began to carefully back toward the mausoleum door. "You find me?" he asked with a nervous chuckle. "I don't even know what you are, never mind who you are."

"I am Archebold," the weird little man in the black tuxedo and tails said. "I'm a goblin."

"Of course you are," Billy said, taking a right turn onto Crazy Street. "Am I supposed to know you?" he asked, hoping to keep the creature talking until he could reach the door.

Archebold shook his head. "Nope, never laid eyes on you before."

"But you've been looking for me?" Billy questioned.

The creature nodded, his smile getting wider.

"Then who am I?" Billy challenged, feeling the cool breeze from outside on his back. He was almost there.

"Don't be silly," Archebold said with a chuckle. He reached behind his long-tailed jacket and produced what looked like a rolled-up comic book from his back pocket.

Billy's eyes widened in horror. A comic book should never be treated like that.

"This is you," Archebold said, shoving the comic into his hands.

The comic book was old, really old, and Billy's eyes immediately absorbed the cover image, reading the title aloud. "*Owlboy.*" Despite his surroundings, he found himself studying the hero running toward him into action on the cover. He'd heard of Owlboy before but had never seen one of the comics. There was actually something appealing about the superhero with his brown and green costume, funky cape that sort of looked like feathers, and cool helmet with goggles.

"I don't get it," Billy said, looking up.

"Can't think of any other way to say it." Archebold moved to stand beside him, and Billy quickly stepped back. The goblin ignored him and jabbed at the book's title with a stubby finger. "You are the Owlboy."

Billy vigorously shook his head as he laughed nervously. "Nope, sorry, you got the wrong guy. I . . . I'm just a kid." He tried to give the comic back, but Archebold wouldn't take it.

"You're joking, right?" the goblin asked.

"Do I look like I'm joking?" Billy put on his most serious face.

"Oh my," Archebold said in shock. "Then when you arrived to rescue me, it was just . . . an accident?"

Billy shrugged. "I heard somebody calling for help and decided to see what I could do."

The goblin stroked his chin, slowly nodding. "Yes, that's it. And even though you didn't realize it, you ran straight into the arms of your destiny."

"Whose arms?" Billy asked, wrinkling his nose, still confused.

Archebold again leaned in close, pointing a sausage-like finger at the comic Billy held. "Destiny's arms," he repeated. "This is your destiny . . . to be the next Owlboy."

"Me?" Billy asked, his voice coming out like a squawk.

Taking hold of his arm just below the elbow, Archebold started to explain. "You are to be the next protector of Monstros City."

"Where?" Billy asked.

Archebold rolled his eyes. "Monstros City," he said slowly. "The world beneath this one." The goblin pointed to the floor, his shaggy eyebrows going up and down.

"There's . . . a world . . . beneath the cemetery?" Billy began to panic. This was nuts. He was standing in a mausoleum talking to a goblin about a city under the cemetery after being attacked by a pig-man.

Check, please!

"Beneath this human cemetery, there exists a fabulous place—a vast city populated by monsters of every shape and size."

"There are monsters underneath the cemetery?" Billy asked in a whisper, nearly certain that his parents had been right. Was this what brain damage was like?

"What else would live in a place called Monstros

City?" The goblin looked a bit annoyed as it shook its oddly shaped head. "Circus clowns?" Archebold started to pull Billy toward the back of the mausoleum. "Don't tell me you've never heard of Monstros City. It's been voted scariest place to live by *NewsShriek* magazine five hundred years in a row. I can't wait for you to see it. . . ."

Inside his head, Billy heard the sound of screeching brakes. No way. He had zero intention of going anywhere near a place called Monstros City . . . especially with a goblin. Without another thought, he yanked his arm from the goblin's grip.

And bolted for the door.

This is nuts, Billy thought, slamming through the mausoleum door, the crazy alarm going off in his head big-time.

The cool air helped to clear his mind, but it didn't make the craziness of the situation go away.

The creepy little creature dressed like he was going to a wedding had said Billy was the next Owlboy. Billy's thoughts raced as he ran down one of the winding paths through Pine Hill Cemetery, his brain going a million miles a minute. Did Archebold know Randy? Could he and Billy's mortal enemy have cooked up a plan to make Billy think he was losing his marbles? Naw, this wasn't Randy's style. Randy was more physical; he would've preferred to beat Billy's head until the marbles just fell out, none of this subtlety stuff.

And then it hit him: what if the entire incident was just the product of his sometimes overactive imagination?

He remembered last summer, when he was certain that invaders from Mars had landed in his neighborhood during a particularly nasty thunderstorm. It was an honest mistake; in the lightning, the electric company repair trucks did look a little like Martian death cruisers.

Billy ran faster, feeling the slap of the cement path through the soles of his sneakers.

Is that it? he wondered. *Or maybe I really did play ball with Randy and Mitchell and they hit me over the head with their bats and now I've got this horrible head injury giving me all kinds of crazy dreams.*

Up ahead, just before the next bend in the path, he saw the stone wall that separated his backyard from the cemetery. If he could just get to his house, he knew he could wake up.

He pushed himself even faster, certain now that this was all just one big, crazy nightmare.

But then how did he explain the Owlboy comic book he was still holding?

He would always blame what happened next on a wet patch of slimy fall leaves, but in fact, the cause was just as likely to have been his own clumsiness born of fear. Whatever the reason, he lost his footing and careened off the path, moving so fast he couldn't stop, until he plowed headfirst into a marble headstone.

Billy had never dreamed that nightmares could be quite so painful.

CHAPTER 2

"You are the Owlboy," the tiny creature screeched, waving the old comic book.

Billy awoke with a start to find himself lying face-down in the grass atop a grave.

"What the . . . ?" he began, pushing himself up to his knees. He felt a bit dizzy, swaying slightly as he brought his hand up to touch the front of his aching head.

He winced, feeling a good-sized bump as well as some sticky wetness. "Oh no," he said, looking at his fingers where a little blood had stained them.

Then, noticing that the cemetery around him was a little out of focus, he looked about for his glasses. He could just make them out lying on the ground near him and picked them up. Checking them first to be sure they weren't broken, he breathed a sigh of relief as he returned them to his face. At least he wouldn't have to explain that to his parents.

As the world came back into focus, he saw the comic book lying on the ground next to him and slowly picked it up. He glanced back down the path toward the Sprylock mausoleum.

Had it really been some kind of waking nightmare? A hallucination? But again, how did that explain this?

Billy stared at the cover of the comic book for a moment, then finally got to his feet, brushing stray blades of grass from the front of his sweatshirt. The sun was starting to go down, and he wondered how long he had been lying there. He was considering going back to the mausoleum, just to prove he wasn't crazy, when he heard his mother's voice.

"Billy! Time for supper!"

He felt a rumbling ache in his stomach and realized he hadn't had anything to eat since breakfast. *I can always check tomorrow*, he told himself, and trudged toward home.

"Coming, Mom!" he yelled.

By the time he'd climbed over the wall and into his backyard, he'd almost convinced himself that the events at the mausoleum had just been some strange, out-of-control daydream. But that still didn't explain the comic book.

He could just hear it now: *Hey, Billy, where'd you get the wicked old comic book?*

A goblin gave it to me in a mausoleum! Maybe he'd be finishing up sixth grade at the Happydale Insane Asylum.

He opened the back door to the kitchen, pondering this disturbing thought, and his mother started to scream.

Billy jumped, whipping around to see if the pig-man, or maybe Archebold, had followed him home, but he saw nothing.

"What?" he screamed back, looking at his mother's wide-eyed face as she stood near the stove, hand clutching her mouth.

"What happened to your head?" she shrieked.

"I fell down in the cemetery," he answered in an equally shrill voice.

"You hit your head?" Mrs. Hooten's eyes bulged and her voice dropped to a troubled whisper.

Billy nodded quickly, afraid to answer. He looked at his dad, whose face was hidden by the newspaper he was reading at the kitchen table. No help there.

"You stay right where you are, young man," his mother ordered, racing out of the kitchen. "Who knows what kind of damage you could've caused!" Billy caught the sounds of her rummaging through the bookcase in the family room.

He knew exactly what she was looking for. Whenever he had a health issue, his mother would break out *Doctor Mellman's Encyclopedia of Old-Timey Cures*, a book she'd picked up at a garage sale before he was even born.

With a sigh, he pulled out one of the kitchen chairs and sat down. He wondered if the cure for this injury would involve rubbing bacon fat over the affected area or drinking a glass of lemon juice while holding his breath and standing on one foot. Those were just some of the old-fashioned remedies that Billy's mother thought worked wonders.

"What happened again?" his dad asked from behind the newspaper.

"Slipped on some leaves and whacked my head on a tombstone," Billy replied.

"You all right?" his father asked, turning the page.

"Yeah," Billy said, shrugging. "Got a cut on my head, but it didn't bleed much. I feel fine."

"Good," his dad said. "Why don't you go get washed up for supper?"

Billy opened his mouth to tell his father about the events at the mausoleum, then thought better of it. *Hey, Dad, you were right, your only son really is insane.*

Instead, he headed for the upstairs bathroom. As he climbed the steps, he could hear his mother return to the kitchen, asking his father where he had gone.

And whether they still had any bacon fat left in the fridge.

That night, no matter how hard he tried, Billy could not fall asleep.

Neither of his old standbys worked: counting the number of things his collection of *Transmogrifier* robots could transmogrify into, or how many unusual ways the Mongoose had tried to kill the Snake. No matter what, Billy couldn't get the bizarre memory of what he had seen that afternoon to leave his head.

The cut on his forehead throbbed, yet another reminder of the most bizarre day ever, and he reached a hand out from beneath the covers to wipe away the excess bacon fat from his mother's—and Dr. Mellman's—remedy. He rubbed his hand on the solar system comforter that covered his bed and turned over, trying to get comfortable.

Was it a hallucination or not? asked a tiny voice in his head, a voice that sounded an awful lot like him doing his mad-scientist imitation.

He sat up, his thoughts racing. He could straighten

his room; he could pull out some back issues of *Snake* and reread them; he could watch some late-night television. But deep down he knew that none of that would silence the question that still rattled around inside his head.

What really happened today?

Billy looked toward his dresser. He had shoved the Owlboy comic book into his underwear drawer on his way to the bathroom to wash up for dinner. Since then, he had avoided his bureau as though it would give him that flesh-eating bacteria. But if he got up right now and took a look, would the book still be there? Or would it have faded away like the bad dream he was praying the mausoleum incident really was?

There was only one thing to do. Billy tossed back the covers, got out of bed and turned on the light. Slowly— carefully—he reached for the knobs of his dresser. Then, holding his breath, he pulled open the drawer.

He smiled, looking down into the drawer at a sea of underwear and socks, and breathed a sigh of relief. It really had been just his mind playing tricks on him. Feeling much better, and almost certain that he could fall asleep now, he started to push the drawer closed.

And that was when his eyes caught a glimpse of something bright yellow peeking out from beneath a navy blue sock.

Billy wanted so badly to simply shut the drawer and jump back into bed, pulling the covers up over his head, but instead he reached into the drawer and flipped over the sock to reveal . . .

The Owlboy comic book.

Strangely enough, a part of him was actually relieved to find it there, because that meant he wasn't losing his marbles. He knew that everything that had happened to him in the mausoleum . . .

Was real.

He slid the comic out from beneath his underwear. Again he found himself pulled into the artwork on the cover. Even though the book was old, the colors were bright and exciting, and Billy felt his heartbeat quicken just the way it did when he visited Hero's Hovel and picked up the latest issue of *Snake*.

It was almost as if the old comic book was speaking to him.

Read me, it seemed to say in a voice that hinted of something incredible.

And Billy did exactly that, dropping to the floor and opening to the first page.

The cover might have been great, but the inside was absolutely amazing. Within seconds, Billy was sucked into Owlboy's fabulously exciting adventures in Monstros City.

The old issue was much bigger than comic books today, with lots more pages and three stories instead of one. And what stories they were.

Preston Peters was by day a star reporter for the *Big City News*—but once he traveled through that magical doorway into the world of Monstros City, he became Owlboy, hero, protector, fighting evil wherever it threatened. And what about Monstros City, the most exciting place in the world, where every kind of creeping, crawling, swimming or flying monster lived?

Owlboy was forced to match wits with the devilish Dr. Disease and his weapons of infection; Garko, the beast that walked like a man; and an invasion of killer robots from the future that wanted to turn Monstros City into their new junkyard kingdom.

By the time Billy finished the comic—and read it again—he was absolutely exhausted. Never in his twelve years had he read a comic book as totally awesome as this one.

And then he remembered the goblin's words. *You are the Owlboy.*

Billy picked himself up from the floor and returned to his bed. He placed the comic on the nightstand, turned off the light and squirmed beneath the covers.

I'm Owlboy, all right, he thought. *I'm the guy who can defeat Dr. Disease by giving him cramps, beat Garko in an ultimate thumb-wrestling competition and thwart the invasion of a fleet of killer robots with the help of my own fleet of Owlbots.*

Yeah, I do that kind of stuff every day.

But as he closed his eyes and drifted off to sleep, the germ of a crazy idea was planted.

What if the goblin was right?

What if he could be Owlboy?

What if?

Billy awoke early Sunday morning, thoughts of old-time superheroes on his mind. He took his glasses from the nightstand, grabbed the old comic book and immediately started to read it again.

It was even better this time.

But even before he'd finished rereading the last story, nagging questions had begun to develop inside his brain.

What exactly did Archebold mean by saying I'm Owlboy? Why would he say something like that? I'm just a kid who gets his gym shorts pulled down around his ankles at least once a month. How could I ever be as cool as Owlboy?

Questions on top of questions, and before his head

exploded, Billy decided there was only one thing he could do. Tossing back the covers, he got out of bed and slipped on his clothes.

He tiptoed to his door and, as quietly as he could, crept down the hallway, hearing his parents' rumbling snores drifting from their room. Once downstairs, he put on the sneakers he had left on a mat beside the back door and slipped outside.

Standing for a moment on the back steps, he listened to the September wind rustling the leaves on the big old oak tree in the yard, amazed at how strangely peaceful it was this early in the morning. Then he took a deep breath of the smoky fall air and headed toward the stone wall. Even with the early-morning sun, it was still creepy in the cemetery, but that just made it more exciting. Billy imagined himself as the hero in one of the old-time scary movies he loved to watch, heading out to kick the butt of some disgusting monster who had been terrifying the countryside.

He smiled. *Wouldn't that be something?* he thought. *To be a real live hero?*

But the closer he got to the Sprylock mausoleum, the tighter the knot in his belly became. Finally he was standing before the great stone structure, a nasty sensation in his back as if somebody was running an ice cube up and down his spine.

He took a deep breath, gathered his courage and pushed the mausoleum door, hearing the screeching whine of the rusty hinges as the door slowly swung inward. The chamber was filled with a dim, flickering light.

"Hello?" he called quietly. Getting no response, he held his breath and entered the crypt, like a bug drawn to a candle's warm glow.

Billy felt a jolt like the zap of a static shock running through his body as his gaze fell upon the goblin lying on the floor of the mausoleum, sound asleep in front of a tiny fire. Slowly, Billy approached the sleeping creature, then started as he noticed that lying beside the fire, its scaled skin a bright red, was a little dragon, its snores producing small gouts of flame that shot from its nostrils to keep the fire burning.

"Cool!" Billy exclaimed, his voice echoing off the stone walls.

Archebold bolted upright, looking around as he wiped sleep from his eyes. The dragon awakened as well, staring at Billy, gray smoke trailing from its nose.

"Hey," Billy said, waving foolishly at the two strange creatures and suddenly feeling very nervous.

"You've come back. I knew you would!" Archebold scrabbled to his feet. "Didn't I say he'd be back, Ferdinand?"

The small dragon nodded, spreading its folded wings and taking flight to soar around Billy's head.

Billy stared in wide-eyed wonder as Archebold's next words echoed through the stone chamber.

"The Owlboy has returned."

The dragon flapped its leathery wings, hovering in front of Billy's face.

"She likes you," Archebold said, making a silly smooching sound with his mouth and motioning for the dragon to join him. "She doesn't usually take well to strangers," he added as he pulled a small sack from the inside pocket of his coat.

"In you go," he instructed the reptile, pulling the bag open. The dragon took one more pass around the boy's head before zooming down into the opened sack.

"Thank you." Archebold pulled the rope, cinching the bag closed, put it back inside his coat pocket and re-turned his attention to Billy.

"You're much shorter than the other Owlboys, but that shouldn't be a problem," he said, circling the boy and giving him a good once-over. "Yes, you should do quite nicely, Owlboy."

"Stop calling me that. My name is Billy."

Archebold stopped in front of the boy and crossed his stubby arms. "Of course, you can be anyone you like in your civilian life."

"Civilian life?" Billy asked. "But . . . but I'm Billy Hooten all the time."

Archebold began to laugh. This one had a sense of humor; he liked that. The other Owlboys were always so serious. "Good one, sir," he said with a wink.

"No, really," Billy continued gravely. "Look, are you trying to say that . . . that Owlboy is real?"

Archebold couldn't believe what he was hearing. "Of course he's real. He was our greatest hero!" he exclaimed. "Monstros' guardian and protector." He shook his head sadly. "But it's been a very long time since there was an Owlboy."

"Why?" Billy asked. "Did something happen to him?"

"One day he was there, fighting the good fight, and then . . ." Archebold paused for effect. "And then he was gone."

"What happened?"

Archebold shrugged. "Nobody knows, and Monstros was plunged into chaos. The criminals were able to gain the upper hand against the city's law enforcement. After all, there's only so much the police can do."

"So there's no Owlboy in . . . in Monstros City right now?" Billy asked.

Archebold sighed heavily. "There hasn't been an Owlboy in over twenty years. My family has served those great heroes of Monstros since the beginning, but

Grandpa Templeton was the last to bear the honor. It was his Owlboy who disappeared. He's never quite gotten over it. Blames himself and all." Archebold shook his head again.

The fire had started to die down, the shadows of the crypt beginning to close in around them. Archebold picked up a few of the twigs and sticks he'd gathered earlier and fed the dwindling flames.

Billy helped. "So what does your father do, if there's no Owlboy?" he asked.

"He drives a bus," the goblin replied, somewhat embarrassed. He sat down in front of the fire and poked at the flames with a stick. "I couldn't stand to see what was happening to the city anymore. Someone had to do something. So I came here."

Billy sat down across from the goblin.

Archebold pulled the stick from the flames, its tip glowing orange, and waved it around like a magic wand. "This is where the first Owlboy was said to have come from, where all the Owlboys are said to be from."

The two were quiet, staring at the fire.

"I came to find a new Owlboy," Archebold said, breaking the silence. "And I believe I have."

Billy did not look up from the fire, his hands shoved into the pockets of his sweatshirt. "I'm sorry, Archebold," he said quietly. "But I don't think so."

The goblin leaped up, running around the fire and plopping down next to Billy. "Yes, yes, you're an Owlboy, trust me," he said urgently. "You have the same eyes."

"How can you tell through the goggles?"

"You have to trust me," Archebold said earnestly. "Goblins know these things."

Billy stood, shaking his head. "No, Archebold, you've got the wrong guy."

"But—"

"Look, I'm no superhero," Billy interrupted. "I'm just a goofy kid who wouldn't know how to be a hero if it bit him on the butt."

"I could teach you," Archebold pleaded as he too stood. "And there would be no butt biting involved."

Billy smiled sadly. "I'm sorry I made you think I'm something I'm not."

Archebold didn't know what to say. *Could I have really been so wrong?* he wondered forlornly. "But you saved me," he said, trying again.

"That was an accident," Billy explained. "If the pig guy hadn't slipped on those bones, we'd both be in his stomach right now." He stopped and looked around then as if searching for something.

"Yes?" the goblin prodded.

"What happened to him anyway?" Billy asked.

"I dragged him back to Monstros." Archebold pointed

to the open stone coffin at the back of the mausoleum, then stretched, wincing as his bones popped and cracked. "Just about ruined my back."

Billy moved over to gaze at the open coffin. "Is this how you get home . . . is this the mystical doorway back to Monstros?"

"I see you've read the comic," Archebold said happily. "Yes, there are stairs in the coffin that lead down to the city. I could take you there."

For a minute, he thought the boy might be tempted to take him up on the offer, but Billy quickly backed away. "No, that's all right," he said. "I need to get home before my folks wake up and realize I'm gone."

The disappointment returned, nearly crushing Archebold beneath its weight. "I understand," he said dejectedly.

Billy started toward the iron door of the mausoleum. "I really am sorry."

"It's fine." Archebold turned his back on Billy and trudged toward the open coffin. He had told his family he was going to the world above to find a new Owlboy, and he felt sick with the knowledge that he had failed.

He had been so sure that Billy was the one.

The goblin hopped up onto the coffin and was preparing to drop down into the darkness when he noticed Billy standing by the door, watching him.

41

Archebold paused for a moment, then jumped back to the ground, reaching inside his coat pocket as he crossed the room. Finding what he was looking for, he tossed something to Billy.

"This is for you," Archebold said, watching as Billy caught the object against his chest.

"What is it?" Billy asked, examining the white owl-shaped object.

"It's a whistle," Archebold explained.

"A whistle?" Billy asked. "What for?"

"Just in case," the goblin said, and he returned to the open stone coffin, jumping onto the edge before dropping into the darkness to return home.

"Just in case."

Chapter 3

The rest of Sunday seemed to last forever.

Even though it was a day off from school—one of the most precious gifts in the whole universe—Billy couldn't concentrate.

He tried watching some of his favorite DVDs, but just couldn't get into them. And trying to play video games was useless; he kept getting knocked out because he could not get Archebold's crazy story out of his head. In fact, things got so bad he committed the ultimate sin—he wished that Sunday was over and that Monday would hurry up and arrive. At least then he'd have something else to think about.

And arrive Monday did.

By the time Billy fell asleep Sunday night, it seemed that his mother was already at the foot of the stairs calling for him to get up and get ready for school. Even though he'd wanted to rush into the first day of the week, Billy barely made it to homeroom before the late bell rang.

His mind was filled with an ugly goblin face spinning tales of how Billy was a superhero in an underground city of monsters. The idea was nuts. So why in the world couldn't he forget about it? *Is it because the idea is so freakin' cool that I don't want to forget it?* he wondered.

His morning classes were torture. He tried to concentrate; he really did. But when Mrs. Doherty was teaching her English class about the proper use of the comma, her voice kept changing, sounding more and more like the goblin Archebold, and soon Billy wasn't hearing anything about commas anymore.

I came to find a new Owlboy. And I believe I have. The goblin's words echoed in Billy's mind.

Finally the bell for lunchtime rang.

Maybe if I eat something, Billy thought, plunking himself down on one of the bright orange plastic chairs in the cafeteria at Connery Elementary School. He fished through his book bag for the brown paper sack containing his lunch, and his fingers brushed against something he didn't even know was there. He pulled his hand out of the bag with a start, staring inside at the old Owlboy comic.

"I thought I left you in my room," he muttered, struggling with the urge to pull out the comic and read it again.

"Are you talking to something in your book bag, Billy?"

Billy looked up to see his friend Danny Ashwell standing at the table, lunch tray in hand. "You know, it's bad enough people think we're geeks, but when you add crazy to the mix . . ."

"Just talking to myself," Billy said, ignoring the comic and pulling out his lunch bag.

Danny placed his tray on the table and sat down across from Billy. "Let me know if the two of you want to be alone."

"Knock it off," Billy ordered. "I've got a lot on my mind."

"Tell me about it," said the heavyset Danny, digging into his macaroni and cheese as if he hadn't eaten in a month. "The science fair is only six months away and I still don't know what my project's gonna be."

Three more of Billy's friends, Kathy B, Dwight and Reggie, showed up with their lunches. They greeted each other in their usual, or unusual, way. Danny grunted, way too busy shoveling food into his maw to be bothered saying hello. Dwight gave everyone his special nod, trying to be the coolest kid at the table but instead looking as if he had a nervous tic.

"Hey," Reggie said with a big grin that showed off the most elaborate set of braces Billy had ever seen.

Kathy B, who hadn't yet taken her seat, appeared to be thinking, and Billy knew exactly what she was about to do, because she did it every day.

Suddenly, she cleared her throat. "Good night, good night! Parting is such sweet sorrow, that I shall say good night till it be morrow," she said in a powerful voice filled with emotion as she gazed up at the fluorescent lights in the ceiling.

The boys glanced up as well, just in case there was something to see.

She looked back down at them. "Well?"

Every day Kathy B would rattle off a Shakespeare quote and wait for somebody—*anybody*—to guess what play it was from.

"*Green Eggs and Hamlet!*" Reggie screamed, and everybody rolled their eyes and shook their heads.

Reggie used the same joke every day, and Billy wondered when he would realize that it was only funny once.

Once.

Kathy B ignored Reggie, taking her seat in a disgusted huff. "It's from *Romeo and Juliet*, you dopes," she said, unzipping her lunch bag.

Yep, it's a veritable geek rainbow at the ol' lunch table, Billy observed. He usually enjoyed lunch with his pals, a gentle reminder that he wasn't the only weirdo in school. But today he didn't feel like joining in as everybody excitedly talked about their weekend activities. The stuff he had to share was just too bizarre, even for this group.

He listened to Danny talk about the moldy half of a sandwich he'd found under his bed on Saturday, and listened to Dwight tell how he'd gone to the coolest birthday party ever and hadn't gotten home until *after* midnight. Reggie talked about how awesome his teeth were going to look once his braces came off—*big surprise*—and Kathy B regaled them with tales of her new production of *Macbeth*, which wasn't going well because her all-cat cast wouldn't stop fighting.

And then it was as if they realized all at once that Billy wasn't talking.

"Hey, what's wrong with you, Billy?" Kathy B asked, popping a corn chip into her mouth and chewing noisily.

"He was talking to his book bag when I got here," Danny said. "I thought maybe he was going insane."

Billy crossed his eyes and stuck out his tongue. "I was hoping you wouldn't notice," he said in one of his weird voices.

Everyone at the table laughed—well, except for Dwight. The face and screwy voice must not have been cool enough.

Reggie tossed a balled-up napkin at Billy, and Billy caught it easily. "What's goin' on? You feelin' all right?" he asked through his mouth of metal.

"I'm fine," Billy assured them. "Just thinking." He reached into his bag and carefully removed the Owlboy comic, laying it on the table.

Everyone seemed properly impressed by the old book, except of course for Dwight.

"Owlboy," Reggie read, his eyes wide as he reached out to touch the cover. "That's an old one," he said, and then started to giggle, looking at Billy.

"What?" Billy asked.

"Is that where Randy got the name?"

"Doubt it," Billy answered. "I don't think he can even read."

"What's it about?" Danny asked as he broke off a piece of double fudge brownie and shoved it into his mouth. "Is it like *Snake?*"

Billy reached out, flipping open the comic. "No, it's really different."

He realized this was his opportunity to see how his friends would have reacted if they had been faced with Archebold and his offer.

"It's about this kid who's been chosen to be this superhero . . . Owlboy, and how he protects this underground city where monsters live, from evil and stuff."

The gang just continued to stare at the brightly colored artwork as Billy slowly turned the pages.

"Sounds neat," Reggie said, clutching a napkin to his mouth. His braces had a tendency to make him drool when he got excited.

"Think so?" Billy asked warily. "What if you guys were chosen to be a hero—would you do it?"

"Depends on the hero," Dwight said, reaching out to turn the comic toward him. "Is this him?" he asked. "He looks okay. I guess I'd do it."

"Me too," Danny piped up, his face covered in chocolate. "Usually, these superhero types have great big laboratories where they do all kinds of experiments."

"Almost as good as being onstage," Kathy B said. "And besides, I like the cape. It's very theatrical."

Billy was both surprised and pleased by his friends' responses. *Maybe this isn't such a crazy idea after all.*

"Well, well, well, what've we got here?" the unmistakable voice of Billy's mortal enemy boomed.

Why was it that whenever Billy started to feel positive about anything, something bad—like Randy Kulkowski—had to come along and ruin it?

Billy reached for the comic, but Randy—being

closer to ape and all—was faster and snatched it up from the table.

"Be careful with that, it's old!" Billy yelled.

The lunch table gasped.

"Owlboy," Randy read, studying the comic. "That's my idea," he complained. "I think I should sue, what d'you think, Hooten?"

"You can't sue anybody, Randy, that's twice as old as you are," Billy said, reaching for his comic even as he wished he'd learn to keep his mouth shut.

Randy pulled the book away, and his pack of goons snickered behind him. "What did you just say?" he asked.

"I said . . . I said, I think you should sue, you'll probably make a million dollars." Billy reached for the comic again, and again Randy moved it away.

"Yeah," he said with a sneer. "That's what I thought you said."

And then Randy attempted the unthinkable—he tried to rip the old comic in half. Billy nearly jumped out of his skin, until he realized that for some reason, Randy couldn't do it.

Randy grunted, tiny veins bulging on the sides of his large head as he strained to tear the book into pieces. Again his sidekicks snickered.

"What're you laughin' at?" he barked, turning toward them. They quickly fell silent.

"Could I, maybe, have that back?" Billy asked as nicely as possible.

Randy snarled, looking down at the old comic book and then at Billy. "Don't you know this stuff will rot your brain?" He crumpled the comic into a ball and tossed it into a nearby trash barrel.

Randy roared with laughter, pushing Billy backward into his chair before leaving the cafeteria with his friends. "See ya around, Owlboy," he said, and they all started to make hooting sounds as they left.

Billy sat, looking down at the floor. He could feel his friends' eyes upon him.

One by one, they got up and left, not knowing what to say. They had all been on the receiving end of Randy Kulkowski's pranks before; it wasn't fun at all.

"Sorry about your comic," Reggie said, just as the bell rang signaling that it was time for everyone to return to class.

Billy stayed at the table awhile longer, waiting for the cafeteria to empty before he finally got up. Slowly, he reached into the large plastic barrel to retrieve his comic book, more than a little afraid of what the fragile old pages would look like now.

He gasped as he pulled the comic from the trash.

It was exactly as it had been before Randy had touched it.

CHAPTER 4

Now he was *really* confused.

Billy had convinced himself that he was no superhero, but after talking to his friends, he couldn't help thinking that his own wimpiness might have prevented him from taking advantage of an amazing opportunity.

"I'm home!" he called as he opened the back door and stepped into the kitchen. He set his book bag on the table and took off his coat, draping it over the back of a chair.

"Hey there, kiddo. How was your day?" Mrs. Hooten asked, coming out of the family room.

Billy noticed that his mother had a cookbook in her hand, another yard-sale find, and he remembered with horror the last meal she'd prepared with the help of such a book. He shuddered as he thought of what she'd called tuna-noodle surprise—boy, had it ever been one.

"It was okay," he said, unzipping his bag and pulling out the Owlboy comic. He began to flip through the pages, picturing himself defeating the bad guys and saving Monstros City.

"Oh, this sounds yummy," said his mom, her attention already back on her own book. She paused for a moment, tapping her chin with a finger. "But I don't think I have any blood sausage."

Billy just shook his head and rolled his eyes. Slinging his book bag over his arm, he started toward the stairs. "I'll be in my room, Mom," he told her. "I've got a lot of work to do tonight."

"Good luck," she called after him. "Oh, hey, wait a minute."

Billy stopped halfway up the stairs.

"Don't forget to do your homework."

"Yeah, Mom," he said, knowing it would be easier just to agree.

He was continuing up the stairs when she called to him again.

"Hey, Billy!"

"Yes, Mother," he answered, not bothering to hide his annoyance.

"This came for you a little while ago." Mrs. Hooten appeared at the foot of the stairs holding up a cardboard box.

"What is it?" He came down the steps and took it from her.

"Haven't a clue," she replied. "There was a knock at the back door and there it was. Didn't even see the delivery truck drive away."

The box was addressed to Billy in a handwriting he didn't recognize, and he eagerly tore into it to see if there was a card inside. There was indeed an envelope. He set the box at his feet and opened it, his breath catching as he read the words scrawled on the card.

Just in case.

He knew exactly who had sent the package.

Archebold.

"Who's it from?" his mother asked, craning her neck to see.

"Just a friend," Billy answered, looking down into the box. "A friend from school."

Mrs. Hooten nodded. "What is it?"

"Y'know, that stuff," Billy said, going into mom distraction mode. "Remember we were talking about the stuff I had to do something with?" He started up the stairs again.

"That's right," he heard his mother say, "the stuff in

the package." She headed back down the hallway to her recipe book. "Dinner should be ready in a bit, hon."

Billy ran the rest of the way up the stairs with his prize. Ducking inside his room, he closed the door behind him and placed the box on his bed. Carefully, he folded back the lid and stared with growing excitement at the leather helmet, goggles and neatly folded brown and green outfit.

It can't be, he thought, reaching down to touch the fabric and then pulling his hand quickly away. Psyching himself up, he reached into the box and took hold of the outfit. He held the jumpsuit out in front of him, his entire body shaking.

The Owlboy costume.

He wanted to try it on—*but should I?* he wondered.

After all, Billy wasn't Owlboy, but why would the goblin have sent it to him if he didn't think there was even the tiniest chance that Billy would want to put the costume on?

Goblins were sneaky like that.

Billy was already taking off his clothes before he fully realized what he was doing. *This is going to be awesome*, he thought, carefully slipping the costume on.

And then he was in the suit, standing in the center of his room and wondering if he should be feeling any different—because he wasn't.

The costume was scratchy and rough against his skin, but that was all right. It wasn't any more uncomfortable than most of his winter sweaters. He zipped up the front, hoping to give it a snugger fit.

It seemed a little big.

He quickly crossed the room and opened his closet to reveal a full-length mirror attached to the back of the door. He stood before it, and if it hadn't been his own reflection he was looking at, he might've burst out laughing.

The costume was *huge*, as if it had been made for someone three times his size. He stared in horror, lifting his arms and turning first to one side and then the other. Scratchy green fabric sagged at his shoulders and elbows, pouched at his butt and pooled around his feet.

"Oh my god, I don't look like a superhero," he said with disgust. "I look like a superdork."

To make matters even worse, his door suddenly opened and his father stepped into the room. Billy immediately reacted, covering his body with his arms and bringing one leg up as if he'd been caught naked.

His father just stood there, a look of confusion on his face.

"Hey," Billy said, slowly bringing his arms and leg down, preparing himself for the inevitable questions.

"Hey," his father said back, looking him over. "Mom says that since she doesn't have any blood sausage,

we're going to get pizza. She wants you to come down and let us know what kind you want." With that, he turned and left the room.

Billy stood there, stunned. Had his father not seen how he was dressed? *But I guess that's a mystery for another time,* he thought. Then he quickly removed the costume, pulling on his clothes again.

"What was I thinking?" he asked himself, folding the costume and putting it back in the box. "I could never be Owlboy; I'm too much of a dweeb."

Billy really didn't feel like talking after the whole costume incident, but his mother chatted away happily at the dinner table, asking him about his day at school.

He didn't want to be rude, so he did his best to answer her questions, trying to match her cheerful tone. Even still, she seemed to get that something was bothering him, and as he helped her clear the dinner table she stopped him, placing the back of her hand on his brow, checking to be sure that he wasn't feverish.

"I'm fine," he said, squirming away from her. But that was really far from the case, and as soon as they had finished cleaning up, he said good night and escaped to his room.

But Billy's night was just beginning. As soon as he

had seen his ridiculous reflection in the mirror, he had known exactly what he was going to do. He had to sneak out again. The costume had to go back to Archebold so that the goblin could find the *real* next Owlboy.

He sat on the end of his bed and stared at the box containing the Owlboy costume. He still felt the sting of embarrassment at how silly he had looked. Glancing at the alarm clock on his nightstand, he saw that he still had some time before his parents fell asleep in front of the television.

It was the same routine every night: they would finish supper and then head into the living room, where they would both promptly fall asleep. It was almost as if the TV gave off some weird kind of sleep ray that they couldn't fight.

Finally, Billy decided he had waited long enough. He grabbed his flashlight from the bottom drawer of his dresser—the junk drawer—and snatched up the box in his arms. Quietly, he left his room and snuck down the stairs, avoiding the creaky third step. He had perfected the nearly silent descent last Christmas, when he'd been able to scope out all his presents before his parents even knew he was awake.

At the foot of the stairs, he peered through the doorway into the living room. It was just as he imagined: television blaring, his mom and dad both sound asleep, their heads slumped to their chests. Neither of them would wake up until it was time to turn off the set and go up to bed.

I've got at least two hours, he told himself as he made his way down the hallway into the kitchen. He grabbed his coat and opened the door, carefully pulling it closed behind him. *This is starting to become a habit*, he thought as he turned on the flashlight and made his way toward the wall at the back of the yard. Resting the box and flashlight on top, he climbed onto the wall, retrieved his stuff and jumped down into the cemetery.

Billy wanted to make this fast. The quicker he got rid of the costume, the sooner he could get the ridiculous idea of becoming a superhero out of his head.

The Sprylock mausoleum loomed eerily ahead of him, the building illuminated in the cold white light of the moon. Box in hand, Billy used his hip to push open the creaky mausoleum door. He stood in the doorway and shone his flashlight around. The room was empty except for the four stone crypts, the only hint that somebody had been there being the charred remains of Archebold's fire. Even the old bones from the broken stone coffin had been cleaned up.

"Okay, let's get this over with," he muttered under his breath, walking toward the stone crypt with the open cover that Archebold had dropped into.

Billy peered over the edge of the coffin, not quite sure what he would find. The shriveled old body of a dead Sprylock *should* have been what he saw, but instead there was only darkness. He shone his flashlight inside, watching as the deep pool of black swallowed up the beam.

How is this even possible? he wondered, resisting the urge to place his hand inside the coffin and feel around for the bottom. Something told him he wasn't likely to find it.

He leaned over the edge. "Hello!" he called out, listening to the sound of his voice echoing back from within. "Archebold, it's me . . . Billy. I've come to give you back the costume. It doesn't fit and I look like a dork in it."

He listened for a response that didn't come.

Probably doesn't know I'm here, he thought.

And then he remembered the whistle.

Billy set the flashlight and box down on top of the coffin and searched his coat pockets. He found some old gum wrapped in a Kleenex, five elastic bands and the head of an action figure he'd discovered last year in the gutter on his way home from school, but no whistle.

"C'mon," he muttered, digging deeper. "I know you're in here somewhere."

And then he felt his fingers brush against it, hidden in the deepest fold of his pocket.

"Gotcha!" he said, snagging the whistle and pulling it out.

Carefully, he brushed away the dust and lint, then brought the whistle to his mouth. He took a deep breath, filling his lungs, and blew with all his might.

Billy had no idea what the whistle would sound like, but he would never in a million years have imagined the sound that did come from it. It was like hundreds of owls hooting loudly all at the same time. And the freakiest thing was—it didn't stop, even after he had taken the whistle from his mouth.

Suddenly, there was another sound, a ghostly moan that he realized was the wind outside only after it had blown the heavy mausoleum door open with enough force to smash it against the inside wall of the crypt.

Billy jumped back, startled by the crack of the door. The backs of his legs hit the lip of the coffin, and he stumbled backward. His arms flailed crazily as he tried to grab hold of something—anything—to prevent himself from falling backward into the open coffin.

But no such luck.

His fingers brushed across the top of the costume box, knocking it into the coffin with him. And Billy fell, tumbling down, down, down.

Into the bottomless dark.

CHAPTER 5

It felt as if he'd been falling for days.

Just when Billy thought there was no end in sight and that he was going to continue to plummet for who knew how long, he hit bottom.

Well, he hit *something*.

One second he was drifting through an ocean of black, the next he hit what felt like a flight of stairs, and after a bit of a tumble he found himself lying on a cold stone floor.

He lay there moaning. It took him a minute to recover from the abrupt landing, but then he realized the continued absence of all light. He couldn't even see his hand in front of his face, it was so dark. Cautiously he reached out, searching.

A light switch would be nice, he thought, fumbling in the dark, but he found nothing.

He didn't even want to think about where he might be. If he had been reading about something like this— *the room of eternal blackness*—in one of his comics, he'd probably think it was pretty cool, but this was different. This was real.

Billy's leg bumped against something in the dark and he just about fainted. Happy that it didn't appear to be alive, or dangerous, he reached down, finding the cardboard box that contained the Owlboy costume.

What would Owlboy do now? Billy wondered. Well, first of all, he doubted that Owlboy would've lost his flashlight, and second . . .

If this had been a cartoon, a lightbulb would have appeared over Billy's head. Eagerly, he tore open the box, his hands fumbling for the goggles. He found them in a corner of the box and slipped them on over his glasses, tightening the strap in the back. Then he reached up and flipped the switch that would turn on the goggles' most special feature. There was a soft hum and suddenly the darkness became as bright as day.

"Wow!" Billy said, finally able to see his surroundings.

He was in a kind of tunnel, the walls made of smooth black stone. Behind him was an archway with a steep set of steps leading up into more darkness. He figured that was where he'd fallen from, and he rubbed his back, still smarting from his tumble.

Ahead of him, the stone tunnel curved. *Can't hurt to take a peek*, Billy thought, his curiosity getting the better of him. *Who knows, maybe Archebold will be waiting for me at the other end.*

But there was no goblin at the end of the tunnel; there was only a wooden door. Billy pushed it open and stuck his head inside what seemed to be a storeroom. There were shelves everywhere, stocked with what looked like ... groceries. He guessed he was in the back room of a store.

He approached the shelves, taking down what looked like a box of cereal. *Captain Wheezy's Crunchy Critters*, he read. *Made with real bugs!*

"Gross."

He put the box back and picked up a jar from the next shelf. It was filled with a thick, light-green fluid. He read the label. *Mama Pussbottom's Special Dinner Sauce. Great with intestines of all kinds!*

Billy thought he might get sick. He couldn't think of a single person he knew who would enjoy cereal made with real bugs or sauce that tasted great over intestines.

But a monster—now, that was a different story.

And then it hit him, and he almost dropped the jar of disgusting sauce.

I must be in Monstros City.

He hadn't even had a chance to wrap his brain around the idea when he heard a commotion from the room beyond. He paused, hoping that it had just been his imagination, or even the wind.

But then he heard it again, a frantic scream for help followed by the sound of smashing glass. He remembered what he had gotten himself into the last time he'd answered a call for help, and he almost turned around.

Almost, but not quite.

When will I learn? Billy scolded himself, running toward the cries.

Cautiously, he opened the door from the storeroom and found himself in a little grocery store, almost like Bob's Market right down the street from his house.

He slipped quietly from the back room, drawn to the sounds of commotion up front. But even with the threat of danger so close, he couldn't help reading the names of some of the items on the shelves as he moved stealthily up an aisle.

Canned Zamm. The only meat product that bites back!

Doc Corpuscle's Instant Blood. Just like the real thing!

Glabrous Appendage Cream. For dry and chapped tentacles.

Stopping at a corner display for Frizzies Bone Chips and Salsa, Billy peered around to the front of the store and almost let out a squeal of shock.

He slapped a hand over his mouth. He had thought pig-men and goblins were bad, but now skeletons, three of them, wearing plastic masks of human faces, were terrorizing a guy who must be the store's owner. The shop guy wasn't any more normal than the three skeletons. He was short and fat, with bright red skin. And, oh yes, his head was on fire.

Billy closed his eyes tight, then opened them again.

Nope, his eyes weren't deceiving him. Instead of hair on the shopkeeper's round head, there were flames shooting out of it, and when Billy listened really close—over the sounds of the skeletons demanding all the money in the cash register—he could actually hear it crackling.

The shopkeeper had opened the cash register and was handing over the money to one of the skeletons. "Here, take it. It's all I have," he said, placing the small pile of paper and change in the skeleton's bony hand.

The change fell through the bones and clattered to the countertop.

"That's it?" the skeleton asked angrily, his gravelly voice muffled by the plastic mask that covered his face. He showed what little money he had to his companions.

"I think he's holding out on us," the second skeleton said.

"Yeah," agreed the third. "Maybe we should give his head a few squirts and then ask him again."

Billy had believed that the three skeleton robbers were carrying guns, but now he realized that they were actually water pistols.

The shopkeeper backed away from the counter, covering the flames of his burning head. "Please . . . I'm telling the truth, that's all I have. Please don't put me out."

They might only have been squirt guns, but it was obvious that they still terrified the poor guy. And that was just wrong.

Billy's anger took over. He remembered all the times Randy Kulkowski had picked on him while his friends sat quietly, hoping Randy wouldn't notice them.

"Leave him alone," Billy said, stepping out of the aisle, not exactly sure what he planned to do, and wishing his mouth wouldn't always get the better of his brain.

The skeletons spun toward the sound of his voice, pointing their water pistols at him menacingly.

"Who the heck are you?" one of them asked Billy.

"Who the heck is he?" another asked the storekeeper.

Flamehead looked just as confused, shrugging in an *I don't have a clue* gesture.

The skeletons grouped together, water guns still aimed at Billy.

"Stick 'em up," one of the three barked, jabbing the gun in Billy's direction, "and you won't get hurt."

At first, Billy was sort of scared, but then it hit him and he started to chuckle. "You're gonna hurt me with that?" he asked. "I don't think so."

The skeletons looked startled.

"Did he just laugh at us, Tibia?" one of the skeletal criminals asked.

"I think he did, Fibula," Tibia replied.

The third skeleton was looking at his water-filled weapon as he stroked his mask-covered chin with a bony hand. "He's got a point, though. These water pistols ain't gonna do nothing to him."

"Then what do you suggest, Patella?" Fibula asked.

Patella tossed the squirt gun over his shoulder. "I suggest we use our hands." The skeleton flexed his segmented fingers menacingly.

Fibula and Tibia disposed of their water weapons in the same fashion. "Sounds like a plan," they said in unison, joining Patella to creep toward Billy.

You've done it now, Hooten, Billy scolded himself, watching in horror as the skeletons advanced. They were almost upon him, their bony hands reaching to grab him, when he instinctively reacted.

He leaped back, out of their reach, but instead of jumping a few feet to avoid the skeletons' clutches, he found himself airborne, flying backward, bouncing off the ceiling and into the next aisle over.

"Whoa!" he exclaimed, landing in a crouch and falling on his butt. "How the heck did I do that?"

"Hey, where'd the kid go?" he heard one of the skeletons ask.

"He made like a hop-frog and jumped over into the next aisle."

"He ain't gonna get away from us that easy," the third growled.

Billy could hear their bony feet clicking and clacking on the grocery store floor as they hurried to get him. Quickly, he got to his feet.

The skeletons came around the corner. "There's the little creep!" Fibula shrieked.

Tensing his legs, Billy jumped again and found himself hurtling through the air across the length of the store. *If I wasn't being chased by skeletons who want to beat me within an inch of my life, this would probably be fun*, he thought, getting ready to land in what looked like the produce department.

Billy touched down with little difficulty this time, and actually had to wait a while for the skeletons to catch up. While he waited, he took a closer look at the bizarre fruits and vegetables that were for sale.

"These look interesting," he muttered, standing beside a display of bowling-ball–sized fruit that looked like giant eyeballs. According to a handwritten sign, they were called PEEPER MELONS.

"There he is!" Patella cried, leading the skeleton gang as they came around the cleaning supply aisle in hot pursuit of Billy.

Billy grabbed one of the peeper melons, took aim and tossed the fruit at his closest attacker. "Catch!" he yelled.

The melon flew as if shot from a cannon, striking Patella dead center and with such force that it caused the skeleton to explode into pieces.

"Did I do that?" Billy asked aloud, staring at his hands in disbelief. It was almost as if he had . . . *superpowers.*

"Hey, fellas, help me out here!" Patella's skull begged from the floor.

Fibula and Tibia were ignoring their fractured friend, slowly backing along the aisle they had come from.

"This is too cool," Billy said, grabbing another peeper melon and hefting it in his hands like the world's weirdest bowling ball.

"Take it easy, pal," Fibula cautioned. "Let's not do anything hasty."

"He's gonna throw another!" Tibia shrieked, turning to run up the aisle.

"Age before beauty!" Fibula said, pushing past his partner.

"I always thought you were better-looking than me!" Tibia cried, desperate to escape.

Billy took careful aim and let the fruit fly. Holding his breath, he watched the melon bounce down the center of the aisle, connecting explosively with Tibia before sending pieces of Fibula flying into the air.

"Strike!" Billy yelled, pumping his fist in victory.

"Hey, guys!" Patella's disembodied skull called from the floor. "I'd really appreciate some help here."

"*You'd* like some help?" Tibia's skull replied indignantly from the floor of the cleaning products aisle. "What about us?"

Billy took a minute to catch his breath, the enormity of what he had just done washing over him like a tidal wave.

I did it, he thought proudly. *I actually managed to save the day.*

Billy Hooten saved the day.

The shopkeeper with the fiery head came running down the cleaning products aisle, push broom in hand.

"Thank you!" he hollered excitedly. "Thank you oh so much!"

He reached the piles of Tibia and Fibula's bones and immediately started to sweep them into one large heap.

"Hey, knock it off!" Fibula protested. "You'll mix our parts up!"

"I don't want his leg bones, he's got leg bones that are twice as fat as mine!" moaned Tibia.

The shopkeeper kept right on sweeping. "Quiet, you two, I've got a mind to throw you in the trash and forget about you." His head burned a darker red now. "Calling the cops is too good for ya!"

Billy was stunned. He'd never seen anything like this before.

"*Pssst!* Hey, kid!" Patella's skull was trying to get his attention, and Billy looked his way. "Help me put myself back together and I'll make you a deal," the bony criminal whispered. "Twenty-five percent of whatever I bring down."

Billy gave the skull his *you've got to be kidding* face and called for the store owner. "Hey, don't forget this one over here!" he said, pointing out the skull.

The monster with the fiery head pushed the big pile of protesting bones up the aisle toward the pile of Patella.

"No! How could ya, kid? I thought we had something here—I thought we had a deal!"

"Well, at least we're together," Tibia said.

"Shut yer yap," Patella barked as all three skeletons were pushed into one heaping bone pile.

The shopkeeper wiped beads of flaming sweat from his brow and leaned against his broom. "Maybe this will teach you not to mess with my store," he said to the fragmented criminals.

He turned his attention to Billy, dropping the broom to the floor and coming toward him. "How can I ever thank you?" he said, reaching out to take his hand, pumping it furiously. "Thank you! Thank you! Thank you!"

"Sure," Billy said, suddenly feeling very self-conscious. "No problem."

"Those miserable bone jockeys have been robbing my store for years," the shopkeeper said, still shaking Billy's hand. "But tonight somebody stopped them . . . you stopped them."

"I really didn't do that much," Billy said, becoming more uncomfortable. "Jumped around, threw some fruit—no big deal, really."

The shopkeeper stepped back, a shocked expression on his round face. "No big deal? Do you know how long it's been since I've felt safe in my own store? Well, tonight I feel safe. You're a hero . . . you're *my* hero." The creature smiled, the flames on his head burning a cheery yellow.

Billy swelled with pride. *Wow*, he thought. *Somebody just called me a hero. Me. Billy Hooten. Unbelievable.*

"Who are you?" the shopkeeper asked. "I've never seen you around here before . . . have I?"

Billy shook his head as the kindly monster stepped closer.

"Those things over your eyes . . . those goggles," he said. And then his eyes grew wide. "I know who you are."

Billy had forgotten that he was still wearing the goggles.

"No, I really don't think—" he started to explain, but it was too late.

"You're *him!*" the shopkeeper screamed. "You've come back!"

"No. No, I'm not him," Billy said quickly. "I think there's been a terrible mistake and—"

"Owlboy has come back!" the shopkeeper bellowed at the top of his lungs.

And that was when Billy decided that he'd had enough. It was most definitely time to go home.

He jumped up into the air, soaring across the store, landing not far from the door that would take him back into the storeroom, and from there to the entrance of the pitch-black tunnel.

The goggles helped him find his stuff—the box containing the Owlboy costume, as well as his flashlight—

and he headed to the staircase, peering up into a darkness so thick that not even the Owlboy night-vision goggles could penetrate it.

Eager to get home, Billy started to climb. He was careful to watch his footing on the eerily dark stairway, and just when he thought he might have to sit down and rest for a bit, he felt a cool, gentle breeze on his face and the smoky smell of fall air in his nose. Soon after, he saw a white light in the distance above him and knew he was close to home.

The white light became the opening to the Sprylock crypt, and Billy climbed from the stone coffin into the mausoleum. He had never been so glad to get home. The evening's bizarre and exciting events were still bouncing around inside his brain, very much the way he had in the monster grocery store.

He'd been gone far longer than he had expected. He darted from the mausoleum out into the cemetery, running as fast as he could in the direction of the wall that separated his yard from the resting place of the dead. If his parents had checked on him before going to bed, he was going to be in some serious trouble. He started to formulate his story, leaving out all the parts about the mausoleum, falling into a stone coffin and ending up in another world, where he fought a gang of skeletons and then was mistaken for Owlboy.

I'll tell them I was sleepwalking, he decided. *That should do it.*

He tossed the costume box over the wall into his yard and followed it. He composed himself, removing the Owlboy goggles and shoving them in his back pocket before climbing the steps onto the porch.

I wonder if I should be crying? he thought.

He was gearing up for an award-winning sobbing spell as he turned the doorknob and entered the kitchen.

Billy was stunned to find the room empty. *This is odd,* he thought, closing the door behind him. Taking off his coat, he listened to the sound of the television coming from the family room. *They should have gone to bed hours ago.*

And then he glanced at the clock above the sink, feeling his breath catch in his throat. The clock said it was less than an hour from when he'd snuck out. But that was impossible. He had to have been gone for at least twice that time.

Billy had to sit down before he fell down. This was all getting to be a bit too much.

He glanced up at the clock again, just to be sure he hadn't read it wrong, and then double-checked the time on the microwave on the counter. Nope, he'd read it just fine, and according to the clocks, the time he'd spent in the other world beneath Pine Hill Cemetery had taken no time at all.

"How is that possible?" Billy muttered, then realized that just as his speed and strength were better in Monstros City, time must also be different. That was the only explanation that made sense.

Needing a drink to calm his nerves, Billy went to the fridge, removed the milk and poured himself a tall glass. He finished it in two long gulps, then put his glass in the sink and grabbed the box containing the Owlboy costume. Silently, he passed the living room, looking in to see his parents as he had left them, still dozing in front of the television.

"Good night, guys," he whispered, and headed up to his room.

He quickly got ready for bed, and even though he was exhausted, he had trouble falling asleep. His brain was buzzing with thoughts of Monstros City . . . of Owlboy.

And of the future.

CHAPTER 6

Billy went to school the next morning with an extra spring in his step.

Nothing can spoil my mood today, he thought.

He hadn't even minded getting up extra early to finish yesterday's homework. In fact, he'd been having a hard time staying in bed, he was so excited. It reminded him of how he felt on Halloween, Christmas and new comic book day all rolled into one.

It felt electric.

The homeroom bell hadn't rung yet, and he saw his pals hanging out by their lockers as they usually did. Billy sauntered over, barely able to contain his excitement. "Mornin', gents, and lady," he said, slipping his backpack off his shoulders and starting to work the combination lock hanging from his locker.

"Hey, Billy boy," Kathy B said, but the others just grunted, looking as though their Xboxes had exploded.

"What's the matter with them?" he asked her as he hung his backpack inside the locker.

"It's Tuesday," she said with a disgusted shake of her head.

At first Billy didn't understand, and then it hit him. It was *Tuesday*—gym day.

He started to feel that old familiar panic, but managed to get it under control. He wasn't going to let anything spoil today.

It wasn't as if he and his buddies had anything against physical education; as a matter of fact, they enjoyed a good game of basketball or softball, and even a little volleyball from time to time. Unfortunately, Coach Pavlis thought those games were for sissies. In his mind, there was only one game that separated the men from the wimps.

Dodgeball.

Billy was sure the game had been invented thousands of years ago by opposing tribes of cave people as a way of solving disputes without having to go to war.

Why else would it have been created? It certainly wasn't because it's fun.

"Maybe we'll get lucky and Coach Pavlis will be out sick today," Billy said cheerily, taking his gym stuff down from the small locker shelf before slamming the door. "Or better yet, Randy Kulkowski."

They all smiled, nodding in agreement.

The game of dodgeball was bad enough, but when Randy Kulkowski played, it became a death sport. Billy shuddered, remembering the day that Killer Kulkowski—what Randy liked to call himself when he was playing the game—threw a ball so fast and hard that when it narrowly missed his targets and bounced off the wall of the gym behind them, its impact actually made a section of bricks fall out onto the floor.

Scary stuff.

The homeroom bell made them all jump. With one final glance at each other, they headed to the classroom.

"Please be out, please be out, please be out, please be out," Reggie started to chant.

Then they heard the voice echoing down the hallway behind them.

"Hey, losers!"

They all turned, almost as one.

Randy stood at his locker at the end of the hall, late but not absent.

"See you all in gym class," he said with an insane cackle, pretending to throw an imaginary dodgeball in their direction.

Billy swallowed with a gulp.

And he'd been having such a good morning.

Gym class was pretty much what he expected, only worse.

Killer Kulkowski and his cronies were vicious, their aim especially good. One by one, Billy watched his buddies go down, some of them even going so far as to throw themselves in front of a shot just to get knocked out of the game. He knew that was probably the smartest thing to do, but for some reason, he just couldn't bring himself to do it. He thought it might have something to do with his visit to Monstros City and what he had done there.

He had actually been a hero last night. Why should he be running from a game? Real heroes didn't run from anything.

Especially a dodgeball!

"Well, would ya look at this," he heard Randy say as he paced back and forth, tossing the bloodred rubber ball from hand to hand. "All that's left is the Owlboy."

His teammates laughed.

"Finish him off, Killer," Mitchell Spivey cheered, and then laughed hysterically.

There's something really wrong with that kid, Billy thought.

He had never been in this situation, always having been knocked out way before the end of the game, and he found that he didn't really care for it. *Is this what it's like to be a hero?* he wondered, watching as Randy . . . *Killer* prepared his next throw.

Standing alone against the forces of evil.

Billy tensed, watching intently as the ball left his enemy's hand. *It would be so easy*, he thought, *to just turn slightly and let the ball graze me.*

Out. End of story.

Any other day and he was sure that would have been perfectly fine, but not today . . . not after Monstros.

Billy planted both his feet as the ball rocketed toward him. Reaching out, he brought his hands together, catching the ball between them. He stumbled back from the force of the throw, the palms of his hands tingling, but he'd caught it. He'd actually caught a ball thrown by Killer Kulkowski.

You could've heard a fish fart in the gym, it was so quiet, and Billy looked around to see everybody watching him.

His friends, as well as other classmates who had once made up his team, stared at him in awe. Danny Ashwell's mouth was open so wide that he'd actually started to drool.

Very attractive, Danny, thanks, Billy thought.

"So what now, Hooten?" asked the voice of evil.

Randy just stood there, waiting. If he was as shocked about Billy's catching the ball as Billy was, he didn't show it.

Mitchell Spivey cackled like a nutjob as Billy eyed them all. Randy stood out in front, the obvious target, silently daring him to throw the ball. Billy knew he didn't have a chance. His throw would be nothing more than a spitball to the troll disguised as a grade-schooler.

"C'mon, Owlboy," Randy taunted, motioning for him to throw the ball.

The gym was quiet except for Mitchell's insane laughter, and Billy knew exactly what he was going to do.

His eyes narrowed as he fixed his target in his sights. He wasn't sure if it was going to work, but he'd never know until he tried. Pulling back, Billy let the ball fly.

Randy was ready, tensed and waiting as he watched the ball sail right past him to hit Mitchell Spivey.

Billy wished he had a camera as the ball ricocheted off the laughing boy's forehead to hit a startled Randy in the back. It didn't hit him hard, but it hit him just the same.

Billy's friends immediately started to clap. He looked over at them, a smile on his face. He knew that aiming for Randy would have been nothing but a waste, so he'd figured he might as well go for the most annoying of his archnemesis's crew and hope for the ricochet.

After his success in Monstros, maybe things were starting to look up, he thought, waving to his cheering classmates.

But Billy should have been paying attention to what was going on with the opposing team. Reggie's eyes suddenly bugged from his head, and he screamed, pointing across the gym.

Billy turned just as Randy let fly with the ball.

He didn't even have time to think about how much it was going to hurt.

It was a little scary, but Billy was convinced now, more than ever, that he *could* be a hero.

Never had he been the subject of so much attention—well, there was that time with the projectile vomiting at the Patriots game—but that wasn't the kind of attention anybody wanted. It seemed that since he'd stood up to Randy Kulkowski and his crew that morning in gym class, the kids and even some of the teachers were looking at him differently.

For the rest of the day he heard their comments. *"Way to go, Billy!"* *"Hear I missed a good game this morning,* wish I coulda been there." "Whaddya got, a death wish?" "Didn't know you had it in ya, Hooten!"

Neither did he.

Ears still ringing, Billy stood on the sidewalk in front of Connery Elementary, trying to convince his mother that it was okay for him to go to the comic book store on a school day. He was more determined than ever to make this Owlboy thing work.

He was using the cell phone that she had given him for emergencies only. He wasn't sure if wanting to stop at the Hero's Hovel before going home was considered an emergency, but he decided it was better to be safe than sorry.

Mrs. Hooten actually seemed relieved to hear that nothing bad was happening, and that was probably why she agreed to let him go to the comic shop—as long as he was home in time for supper.

The Hero's Hovel was a good half hour's walk from school, but Billy didn't mind; it would give him time to really think about what he was going to do.

His parents had always said he could be anything he wanted to be in life; if he really wanted it and worked really hard, anything was possible.

Billy wondered if being a superhero was one of those things.

First things first, though. He had to learn more

about Owlboy. He needed to become familiar with the costumed hero and the world he protected, and what better way to do that than to read more of his adventures?

And there was only one place in town where he could get his hands on that information—the Hero's Hovel.

The Hovel was in downtown Bradbury, between Barbara's Beauty Salon and Uncle Sal's Hotdog Emporium. A bell chimed cheerily as he pushed open the door and entered his favorite place.

Billy did what he always did when entering the Hovel: he closed his eyes and took in a deep breath. There was something strangely comforting about the smell of the store. It was kind of a musty smell, one that could only be found among old comic books. To Billy, there wasn't a better smell in the world. It was an exciting smell, a hint of the adventure and excitement to be found inside the thousands of old and new comics.

The store's owner was named Cole. He was a big guy, probably around Mr. Hooten's age, with long gray hair, really thick glasses and, always, a Hawaiian shirt. Although he didn't seem to be completely blind, he was always in the company of his Seeing Eye dog, Claudius.

Today, Cole sat on a high stool behind a large glass

counter, his German shepherd lying faithfully beside the chair. The owner was bagging and pricing back issues, using a special guide that told him how valuable the comics were. He had to hold the guide very close to his face to see the listings.

He grunted something that could've been "Howzit going?" as he glanced in Billy's direction and then back to his work. Claudius woofed his own greeting, as he always did. Cole wasn't the friendliest of people. He was perfectly content to sit behind the counter, marking comics and listening to rock and roll music from the eighties, the same kind of music that Billy's parents liked.

The store was a good size, laid out in multiple aisles, each row filled with boxes and boxes of comics. On the walls were hung even more books: special issues, valuable because of their age, or because they contained the first appearance of a popular character, or even because they were drawn by a particularly famous artist. Billy could never afford the wall books, but he always scoped them out just in case he ever found himself with some extra cash.

He didn't know where to start, so he wandered up and down the aisles, taking it all in, trying to figure out where the Owlboy comics might be. He didn't think the company that used to put out the comic book was even around anymore, and the book was so old that there probably wouldn't be a special bin for it.

Finally, Billy realized that he had to ask Cole about the Owlboy comics, but he didn't want to disturb the store owner. He remembered a time a few weeks ago when Cole had actually yelled at a kid for asking him a question about Captain Mighty's powers. It really was a stupid question, though. Everybody knew that Captain Mighty's X-ray eyes couldn't see through lead. Even still, the idea that Billy might suffer the wrath of Cole was almost enough to make him forget about it.

Aw, suck it up, he told himself, and slowly made his way toward the glass counter. *If you're going to be a superhero, talking to scary store owners is going to be the least of your worries.*

Billy stopped in front of the counter and waited to be noticed, but Cole just continued to work. Claudius, however, had risen to his four feet, eyeing Billy over the top of the glass. The dog knew he was standing there, but what about Cole? Maybe he just didn't see Billy.

The man continued to work, holding comic book after comic book up to his face, looking up their value, then slipping them into snug plastic sleeves and marking them with a price sticker.

Finally, Billy cleared his throat.

Claudius looked nervously at his master and back at Billy, who was seriously considering backing slowly toward the door when the man spoke.

"Got a question?" he asked, sliding an issue of *Tales Too Disturbing to Tell*—a comic that Billy's mother refused to let him read because it was too disturbing—into a protective bag.

"Yes, sir," Billy answered, his voice coming out in a nervous squeak.

Cole kept right on working, giving no indication that he had even heard him.

"I . . . I was wondering." Billy began again. "I was wondering if you had any Owlboy comics?"

Cole stopped his work for a moment and glared at Billy, his eyes magnified through the thick lenses of his dark-rimmed glasses. "Owlboy?" he repeated, then laughed disdainfully, and with a shake of his shaggy head went back to work. "You don't want Owlboy, kid," he said, taping a bag shut. "That's old-school stuff, way before your time. I seriously doubt that Owlboy would be flashy enough for you. Why don't you try *Furious Furies*, or *Snake?*"

"No, thank you," Billy said politely. "I already have a bunch of those. I really am looking for Owlboy." He grabbed his bag from where he'd left it by the door and pulled out his new prized possession. "Y'see, I got this comic and I liked it a lot, and I'd like to read some more issues." He held out the book to Cole.

Claudius moved out from behind the counter to take a look. Billy showed it to him, and the dog sniffed the cover. "Don't get any dog boogers on it," he warned the German shepherd. "It's really old."

The dog began to bark wildly, as if insulted. Billy jumped back, not sure what Claudius might do.

"What've you got there?" Cole asked. He'd stood up and was leaning over the counter, a large hand reaching for Billy's prize.

"It's an Owlboy comic," Billy said as Claudius continued to bark.

"May I see it?" Cole asked, almost nicely, and Billy handed the book to him.

As soon as Cole had the comic, Claudius stopped barking, but his tail continued to wag furiously.

"You're right, Claude," Cole said, bringing the book up close to his magnified eyes. "It *is* one of mine."

The statement startled Billy. "One of yours?" he asked. "Are . . . are you saying the book was stolen?"

He started to panic. He'd never even thought to ask Archebold where he had gotten the comic. No wonder the goblin gave it away!

"Where did you get this?" Cole asked, shaking the old comic at Billy.

"A friend gave it to me!" Billy blurted out. "He's not from around here and I didn't think he'd ever even been to your store and . . ."

Cole stared at the comic's cover again before he started to flip through the pages.

Billy was terrified, imagining how much trouble he'd be in when his parents had to go to the police station to get him out of jail. He was about to explain to the store owner that this was all some kind of horrible misunderstanding, when Cole looked up, his big bug eyes boring into Billy's.

"So, what'd you think?" he asked.

"What did I think of what . . . sir?" Billy asked, momentarily confused.

"The comic," Cole said, showing the open book to him. "What did you think of the comic? Did you like it, or did you think it stunk up the joint?"

"It was wicked cool," Billy answered, almost tempted to share with the shop owner that it was based on real-life things, but he knew that would likely get him tossed out of the store for being a wise guy.

"I've seen you in here before, right?" Cole asked.

Billy nodded quickly.

"You like the Snake. Was it as good as an issue of *Snake*?"

"Even better! That's why I'm looking for more issues."

Billy had to fib a little there. He didn't think telling the store owner that he wanted to use the old comics to learn how to *be* a superhero would go over so well.

"Hmmm," Cole said, handing the comic back to him.

"I didn't steal it, sir, I swear," Billy told him. "But if it's yours, you can take it back." He held the book up to Cole.

But the man just laughed, his large belly jiggling up and down. "I know you didn't steal it, kid," he said. "That's not what I meant when I said it was mine."

Billy was confused.

Cole looked around, as if checking to see if he was being watched.

"Can you keep a secret?" he asked conspiratorially.

"Sure," Billy said, and shrugged.

"Keep an eye on the store," Cole told Claudius, and the dog woofed as if to say, *Gotcha, boss.*

The store owner motioned for Billy to follow and led him through the store to the back. They stopped at a door marked PRIVATE.

"You sure you're ready for this?" Cole asked him, one hand on the doorknob.

Billy wasn't really sure what to expect. "I . . . guess," he said.

"Remember, you promised me you could keep a secret," Cole reminded him, and turned the knob.

The door swung open into a darkened room, and Billy squinted, trying to figure out what exactly he was seeing. For a minute, he wished he had his Owlboy goggles, but then Cole reached over and flipped a switch on the wall, and the room was illuminated by the glow of fluorescent lights.

Billy's eyes bulged. "Awesome," he whispered as he stepped into the room for a closer look.

"Yeah," Cole said proudly. "Thought you might think so."

His mother didn't like him to drink Zap cola, but Billy took a big gulp of the ice-cold soda anyway, feeling it fizz in his throat as he drank it down. He smacked his lips eagerly, staring at the bright yellow label with the crackling lightning bolts.

"I never saw Zap in bottles like these before," he said to Cole, who was taking a swig of his own drink.

"It's 'cause they don't make it anymore," the shop owner replied. "When I heard they were going to cans, I bought up a bunch of cases, and I break out a bottle every once in a while on a special occasion."

Billy had some more Zap, looking around the big room for what could have been the thousandth time. The back room of Hero's Hovel was like a museum dedicated to Owlboy. There were posters and toys and pages and pages of comic book art framed on the wall. Billy had never seen anything like it before.

"So is this a special occasion?" he asked as he stood and walked around again.

"Yeah," Cole said, thinking for a minute. "I guess it is. It's not every day that somebody comes in asking about a character I didn't think anyone—especially a kid your age—would remember."

"I only read about him in one of my comic book hero encyclopedias," Billy said, admiring a small toy car that could only have been the Owlmobile. "But when my friend gave me the comic . . ."

Billy looked to see that Cole was smiling, his big round eyes practically twinkling behind the inch-thick glass.

"He *is* a cool character, isn't he?" Cole asked.

"He's awesome," Billy agreed, flipping through some Owlboy comics, some of the oldest comics he had ever seen, in a box on the counter.

"Every time I penciled an issue, it was like the very first time," Cole said dreamily, taking another big swig from his bottle of Zap. "I never got tired of drawing Owlboy's adventures."

Billy heard the sound of screeching brakes inside his head. "What do you mean, you never got tired of drawing Owlboy?"

Cole pointed to the framed art on the walls. "Where do you think I got all these original pages?" he asked. "Sure as heck didn't buy them, would've cost me a fortune."

"You . . . you drew these?" Billy moved around the room again, carefully examining the framed art. "You drew Owlboy?"

"Yep, for almost ten years," Cole said proudly. "Best darn job I ever had."

"That's what you meant by my comic being one of yours—you drew it."

"Bingo!" Cole exclaimed.

"This is amazing," Billy gushed, not sure if his excitement was real or if it was simply the Zap cola kicking in. *No*, he decided, looking at the comics and artwork in the room with new eyes. *This is truly amazing.*

"I can't believe you draw comic books," he continued. "That's gotta be the most awesomest job in the whole world."

"It was," Cole agreed. "Well, until the publisher disappeared and Monster Comics went out of business."

"What happened to him?"

Cole shrugged. "Nobody knows. His name was Preston Stickwell. He was also the creator and writer of the Owlboy adventures, so when he went away, the company and Owlboy went right behind him."

"That stinks," Billy commented.

"Certainly does," Cole agreed. "It's funny, I tried drawing comics for some of the other, bigger publishers, but it just wasn't the same. There was something really special about Owlboy, almost as if he were real or something."

Billy felt the truth bubbling around inside him. He wanted so badly to tell Cole what he had done in Monstros, how there really used to be an Owlboy.

How there might be an Owlboy again.

"Course, then my eyes got bad, and I couldn't do it anymore even if I wanted to," Cole said in a voice tinged with sadness. "But those are the breaks."

Billy didn't know what to say.

As if sensing the sudden change in his master, Claudius wandered into the room and rested his head on Cole's thigh, whining softly.

"Figured if I couldn't draw comics anymore, I could at least sell them," Cole continued, absently stroking the dog's large head. "And the Hero's Hovel was born."

"You miss it, don't you?" Billy asked.

Cole nodded. "More than you know, kid. More than you know."

The silence was becoming uncomfortable, and Billy glanced toward the big windows at the front of the store. The sun had started to go down, and he remembered his mother's warning.

"Well, thanks for showing me all your Owlboy stuff," he said, finishing off the last drop of his soda. "But I need to get going."

"Hey, kid, it was my pleasure," Cole said, taking Billy's empty bottle and placing it with his own in a wooden box in the corner of the room.

Billy had just started to walk out of the room when he heard Cole call to him. He turned back to see the shop owner walking toward him carrying a small white box.

"Here," Cole said, putting the box in Billy's arms. "These should fill you in on just how cool a character Owlboy was."

Billy put the box on the floor, removed the lid and looked inside. He felt his heart do a little dance as he saw dozens of issues of *Owlboy*.

"Wow!" he exclaimed, thumbing through the books.

"You can't have them," Cole warned him. "They're my personal copies. But you're welcome to borrow them, just as long as you promise to keep them in mint condition."

"I sure will," Billy said. "Thanks!" He hefted the box into his arms and left the store, feeling luckier than a hundred-million-dollar lottery winner.

Carrying the box in his arms and his book bag on his back, Billy walked home faster than he ever had before.

Ordinarily, he would have stopped and rested, but just the thought of what was in the box was enough to keep him moving.

Finally, dinner was over and Billy had the rest of the evening to himself. He switched on the ceiling light as he entered his room. He had a lot to do tonight. If this whole Owlboy thing was going to work, something had to be done about the costume.

"Heroes do not look like they're wearing a diaper," he muttered to himself.

He went back into the hallway and rummaged through the linen closet, looking for his mother's sewing kit. He'd goofed around with sewing last year; unfortunately, what was supposed to be the greatest alien invader costume ever built by human hands somehow ended up looking like the Easter Bunny's evil twin, with tentacles. No matter, he was just going to have to get better to make this Owlboy costume work. He hauled out the white plastic sewing kit and returned to his room.

Then his eyes fell on the box of comics on the floor.

"I'll read one comic now and then work on the costume," he decided aloud, eagerly lifting the cover from the box and removing the first book.

"Wow," he said, his eyes taking in the illustration on the cover. It was Owlboy fighting a giant mechanical gorilla. *Can Owlboy defeat the mechanical menace from beyond time?!*, the cover read, and as Billy gingerly removed the comic from its plastic bag, he certainly hoped so.

Soon he was lost in the world of Owlboy again. Owlboy *was* better than the Snake. In fact, Owlboy was probably the greatest superhero Billy had ever read about. This guy had it all: he wore a cool costume and lived in a city loaded with monsters, and he had a secret headquarters called the Roost, all kinds of cool inventions of his own creation and an awesome yellow car that was shaped like an owl's head.

What wasn't there to love? This guy was rad, and if all went according to plan, Billy would soon be having these adventures for real.

One comic turned into two, and more followed. Billy just couldn't get enough of his new favorite hero. Then suddenly, unexpectedly, the comics came to an end. And to make matters worse, the last story was a cliff-hanger.

Had Cole really forgotten to give Billy the last chapter of a story that had the hero in hot pursuit of the master of mind control, the Brainworm, who had managed to take over the Monstros City police force and turn them against Owlboy—or had something far more sinister occurred? Billy double-checked the box and then flipped through the comics he'd already read, thinking he might have mixed them up.

Finally, he remembered what Cole had said about Monster Comics and how the publisher had mysteriously disappeared. Was it possible that the last part of the story had . . . never been published?

He couldn't even begin to think of anything quite so horrible. It was bad enough to have to wait a month for the next issue of a comic, but to be waiting for an issue that would never come?

It would be torture. Pure, never-ending torture.

Billy sat on the floor, his back against his bed. He wasn't sure how long he had been like that when there was a knock at his door.

"Come in," he said softly.

His mother opened the door. "What's the matter?" she asked. "You look like you just lost your best friend."

"I might as well have," he answered, hauling himself to his feet and slipping the comic back into its protective cover.

"Oh, I'm sorry. Anything I can help with?"

"Naw," Billy said, showing her the comic as he placed it back in the box. "Not unless you can find the missing publisher of Monster Comics and get him to tell you how this story ends."

"Nope, can't do anything about that, but it is late," she said. "Dad and I are going to bed. Lights out in ten minutes, kiddo."

"Sure, Mom," Billy said as he made a move toward his bed.

His mother blew him a kiss and closed the door.

Billy waited a moment to be sure his parents had really gone to bed, then went to work.

He laid the costume out on his bed, giving it a thorough once-over. The arms and legs definitely needed to be shortened, and something had to be done with all that excess material in the butt.

He went to the computer on his desk and got on the Internet, finding what he needed on a site called Belle of the Ball after clicking on the article, "Making the Perfect Party Dress with Eloise." All he had to do was somehow adapt the instructions to fit a superhero costume instead of a party dress. Simple.

Yeah, right.

Printing out the instructions, Billy laid the pieces of paper on the floor in front of him and went to work. Sewing was harder than long division and nuclear physics combined, and he was tempted to throw up his hands and quit at least fifty-six times, but he kept going, nearly certain now that this was a test, all part of becoming Owlboy.

A test that he wasn't about to fail.

Billy continued to tape, cut, stitch and hem until, just before sunup, bleary-eyed and barely able to hold the needle, he completed the alterations. He was so tired that he couldn't even be excited. Instead, he simply wrapped himself in the finished costume, lay down on the floor of his room, and fell immediately into a deep sleep.

Billy entered homeroom dressed in his Owlboy costume.

He wasn't quite sure why he was dressed that way, but it felt right. Crossing the room to get to his desk before attendance was taken, he glanced at the clock on the wall, checking to see how late he was.

The black hands on the clock were spinning around as if time was passing by at an incredible speed.

"I think there's something wrong with the clock," he said, turning to look at Mrs. Buchanan, his homeroom teacher, who had for some reason turned into a chimpanzee wearing a pink cashmere sweater, lipstick, pearls and a blond wig.

"Don't look at me," the chimp said, still sounding an awful lot like his homeroom teacher. "I just work here."

And then the entire classroom started to laugh, and Billy turned from the somewhat attractive monkey—as far as monkeys go, anyway—to see what the joke was.

They were all laughing and pointing at him.

At the costume.

Billy adjusted the goggles on his face and stood tall, puffing out his measly chest.

"Is something funny?" he asked, attempting to sound authoritative.

"You're funny," Danny Ashwell said, suddenly producing an enormous sandwich from inside his desk and starting to devour it.

Billy was confused by his friend's words, but the others would soon help explain them.

"Who do you think you are, Billy?" Reggie asked, his braces glistening wetly in the fluorescent light of the classroom. "I hope that just because a goblin told you you were Owlboy, and you fixed some old costume, you don't think you're some kind of hero."

Billy was shocked, and maybe a little hurt, by his friend's words.

"But I went to Monstros . . . and stopped a robbery," he started to explain. "And . . . and I was the last one standing in a game of dodgeball against Killer Kulkowski and . . ."

Kathy B was the next to speak. She stood up from her desk, cleared her throat and looked as if she were about to deliver one of the Shakespeare sonnets she had memorized.

"You are not a hero, Billy Hooten," she said with

precise pronunciation and power in her voice. "You're just a dork in a costume."

Billy was crushed. Even Kathy B didn't believe in him!

He looked to Dwight, who gave him a thumbs-down, and Billy felt the costume begin to change on his body. The sleeves grew longer, the legs of the suit spilled over the tops of his boots, and he could also feel that there was an awful lot of room in the butt.

"But I fixed this," he said aloud, struggling to roll the sleeves back so they didn't cover his gloves. "I worked all night so it would fit me right."

They were all laughing at him again, and he didn't know whether to go to his seat and just suck it up or leave the room—leave school and just go home for the day to rethink this whole hero business.

Suddenly, the room began to shake.

Billy stumbled to the right, grabbing hold of Mrs. Buchanan's desk so he didn't fall. The room became eerily silent, and everyone looked up to the ceiling—except for Danny, who was still eating his really big sandwich.

"What's going on?" Billy asked.

"Don't ask me," said the chimpanzee, adjusting the blond wig on its head before going back to its crossword puzzle. "I just work here."

And with the monkey's last words, the roof of the school was torn away with a sound like the worst thunderstorm Billy had ever heard, only ten times louder, exposing the class to the dark, open sky—and something else.

Something horrible.

It was a monster, a giant two-headed beast, shaggy and green, that held the roof of the school in one of its enormous paws while glaring with its four blood-shot eyes down into the school, admiring the kids of Billy's homeroom as if they were a freshly opened box of chocolates.

"Yum," the two heads said in unison, tossing away the roof of the school. Both heads licked their lips eagerly.

This is my chance, Billy thought, feeling the power of heroism flow through his body. This was his opportunity to prove to his friends that he could do the job— that he was indeed a hero.

And suddenly the costume didn't feel quite so big anymore.

The dual-headed beast reached down into the class-room with a giant green hand for Danny Ashwell, who really didn't seem to notice that he was in danger. It was all about the sandwich with Danny.

"Wait!" Billy screamed in his most heroic voice.

And the monster did wait, pausing before plucking Danny from his chair.

"Don't you dare touch that child!"

The two horrible faces of the giant creature began to smile, and Billy felt something that could've been a large rock—or maybe even a dodgeball—form in the pit of his stomach.

He knew the monsters—their faces. They looked exactly like Randy Kulkowski and Mitchell Spivey.

"And who are you supposed to be?" asked the beastly Randy. Right on cue, the one that looked like Mitchell began to laugh that horrible cackling laugh.

It was bad enough to hear the normal-sized Mitchell doing it, but a giant Mitchell? It was enough to make Billy want to jam pencils into his ears. Really hard.

"I'm . . . I'm . . ."

Billy didn't know if he *wanted* to say it . . . if he *could* say it.

"What's the matter?" the Kulkowski beast asked. "Owl got your tongue?"

Again Mitchell laughed. Billy had pretty much had enough.

"I'm *Owlboy*," he proclaimed, and found that it really didn't feel all that bad rolling off his tongue. He'd almost started to believe that he could pull this off, when it all went horribly wrong.

Isn't it always the way?

The Randy-Mitchell twins produced two enormous pieces of bread and reached for Billy. All he could think was *Where the heck did they find bread that big?*

He tried to bat the huge, badly-in-need-of-a-manicure hand away, but the monster was too fast. Monstrous fingers wrapped around him in a powerful grip, yanking him from in front of Mrs. Buchanan's desk. His last sight before being hauled up into the air was the chimp sitting there, filing its nails.

"Don't look at me," it said yet again, completely unfazed by what was going on in the classroom. "I just work here."

Billy found himself dropped onto the squishy surface that was one of the giant slices of bread.

"You ain't Owlboy," the Randy beast said before placing the other slab of bread on top of him.

Billy struggled beneath the top slice.

"Nope, you ain't Owlboy at all."

Billy managed to partially squirm his way out from between the twin slices, peeking over the top of the bread as it was on its way to the monster's open mouth.

"You're lunch," the Randy monster said.

Just before taking a really big bite of his Billy Hooten sandwich.

* * *

Billy woke up on the floor of his room, the rough material of the Owlboy costume wrapped around his head, muffling his girlish scream.

"Oh, jeez," he said, pulling the costume from his face, his eyes darting around the room, searching for any sign of the Randy-Mitchell beast. He felt the top of his head, just to be sure that it hadn't been eaten.

"Billy!" he heard his mother call from the bottom of the stairs. "Time to get up, pal. Let's shake a leg!"

"Okay, Mom!" he replied, trying to keep from freaking out.

He got up from the floor, a little shocked to see that he was still wearing his clothes from yesterday, and then remembered how he had spent the entire previous night and how hard he had worked. He snatched up the costume from the floor, holding it by the shoulders at arm's length.

Memories from the freaky dream flooded his mind: his closest friends telling him that he could never be a hero, never be Owlboy, and then the fact that he had become the meat in a giant sandwich. At that moment, Billy wasn't feeling very confident and was tempted to fold up the suit, put it back inside the box and throw it way in the back of his closet where it couldn't be seen.

But then he remembered the crazy grocery store in Monstros City and how good he had felt when the shopkeeper had thanked him.

"Billy!" his mother called again from downstairs. "Are you ready, kid?"

He smiled.

Yes, he was ready.

CHAPTER 7

The next couple of days were torture. Billy couldn't wait for school to be over.

He had big plans for Friday night—*monster-sized plans.*

He could barely hold in his excitement. Whenever one of his pals asked him what he was doing for the weekend, it was all he could do not to start babbling about putting on his costume, heading to Monstros City and becoming Owlboy—for real.

So he just smiled uneasily and told them . . .

"Nothing special."

Billy had no idea what the weekend had in store for him. He knew that he was going to Monstros on Friday night, and hoped that if he didn't screw up too badly, he'd be allowed to go back on Saturday and maybe even Sunday, too. But he would have to see.

The last bell on Friday was like the firing of a starter's pistol. Billy was gone in a flash, gathering up from his locker all the stuff he would need for school-work over the weekend and heading home with only one thing on his mind.

His journey back to Monstros City. And this time, he would be ready.

If Billy had thought the last few days of school were bad, that night at home was at least fifty times worse.

Friday nights were always special at the Hooten house. His father would pick up takeout from the Chinese Dragon and a movie from the Video Vault downtown. Billy usually loved Friday nights: gorging himself on spicy General Tso's Chicken and heaping piles of the house specialty fried rice, followed by a movie, usually something filled with lots of violence and explosions, because his dad loved movies like that. But tonight, he couldn't wait for the leftovers to be put away and the movie started so that he could get his own special night underway.

"Think you're gonna like this one, Bill," his dad said, eyeing the DVD package. The movie was something with that big dude with the weird accent, and Billy was certain they had seen it at least four times over the last year, but his dad loved the movie and would pretend he didn't remember seeing it.

Which in a way was probably sort of true.

Friday movie night wasn't much different than any other night at the Hooten household, in that once the movie was put inside the player, it wasn't too long before his parents were watching a different kind of movie—the one playing on the inside of their eyelids.

But for some reason, tonight was different.

Billy sat stiffly on the loveseat, waiting for his parents to doze off, but they didn't. His father sat attentively in his recliner, a big stupid grin on his face as he watched the muscle-bound dude wipe out a hundred bad guys without ever reloading his gun. Billy's mom was curled up in the corner of the couch wrapped in her favorite comforter, busily working on a crossword puzzle.

This is insane, Billy thought, unable to ever recall a time when his parents hadn't been asleep fifteen minutes into the movie. *Tonight of all nights.*

He was very close to losing it when he saw the first signs that things were about to take a turn for the better.

Gazing down into her puzzle book, his mom was the first to go. Billy watched as her head began to dip, the grip on her pen going limp. It wasn't long before she was out like a light.

His dad was fighting it; like the action hero in his movie, he was doing battle with the nefarious villain sleep, which was attempting to pull him down into its clutches.

Billy sat tensed at the edge of the loveseat, waiting for his dad to give in. He was almost tempted to start singing a lullaby to help him along, when at last his father's eyes closed, and within seconds he was snoring.

Springing up from his seat, Billy did a little dance of excitement, making his way from the room and bounding up the stairs to get ready.

Tonight was the night.

Slowly, Billy dressed.

First it was the jumpsuit. He put it on carefully, not wanting to pop any of the new stitches. *Not bad,* he thought, moving around a bit. He craned his neck, trying to get a good look at his butt.

Not bad at all. Eloise would be proud.

The boots and gloves were next. The ones that the costume came with weren't even close to being his size, so he'd had to improvise, taking a pair of old winter boots from his closet and painting them a dark green. The gloves had proved to be a little more of a problem. He hoped his mom didn't need them to weed the garden anytime soon, but doubted that she would have remembered where she'd left the heavy green gloves anyway.

The leather helmet and goggles were last, and his hands were shaking a little as he put the helmet over his head and then slipped the goggles on over his glasses.

It was the moment of truth, and Billy felt himself start to break out in a sweat that had more to do with nerves than being hot. He approached his closet door and, counting to ten, swung it open to see his reflection.

He was stunned at first, but slowly—gradually— he became used to the idea. *Will you look at that?* he thought as a smile crept across his face. *Owlboy's in the house.*

Hands on his hips, Billy struck a heroic pose and was shocked at how cool he looked.

"Oh, Owlboy, how will the citizens of Monstros City ever repay you?" he said in a high-pitched voice.

"No need to thank me, my good lady . . . squid thing . . . person," he responded in his best superhero voice, not a hundred percent sure of how to address them. That was something he'd have to ask Archebold.

Billy looked at himself from every angle and was still impressed by what he saw.

"You are one handsome devil, Billy Hooten," he said to his reflection. "How'd you get to be so darn good-lookin'?"

Finally able to pull himself away from the mirror, Billy made sure he had everything he needed. Before he was finally ready to leave the house, he had gone back multiple times to the box that Archebold had sent him.

Billy left his room, closing the door to give the impression that he had gone to bed, just in case his mom checked on him later. Creeping down the stairs, avoiding the noisy step, he peeked into the family room to be sure that his parents were still asleep and where they were supposed to be. His mom had curled herself into the corner of the couch and had wrapped herself even more tightly into the cocoon she'd made from the comforter. His father's head was leaned back now in the recliner, his mouth agape, making a noise that was part enraged water buffalo and part clogged bathtub drain.

Excellent, Billy thought, ready to sneak from the house, when the unthinkable happened.

His father lifted his head, smacked his lips and blearily looked around the room.

Billy froze, waiting for the world to come crashing down around his ears. *How can I possibly explain this?* he wondered feverishly. *It would be impossible, even for an out-of-the-box thinker like me.*

His father looked directly at him and Billy prepared for the worst.

"Hey, Dad," he said, wondering if his father would recognize him all decked out in his superhero attire.

"Thirsty," his dad mumbled, still smacking his lips and looking around the room as if he'd never been there before.

Billy was shocked. His father didn't seem to notice that he was standing there dressed like something out of a comic book.

"Would you like me to get you something . . . some water, maybe?" Billy asked softly, certain that his dad was still in some kind of weird sleep state.

"Water," his father replied, struggling to keep his eyes open. "Water'd be good."

Billy ran from the room, his short cape flowing behind him as he went to the refrigerator and found a bottle of water. He quickly brought it back to his thirsty, semiasleep dad.

"Here ya go," Billy said, opening the bottle before handing it to him.

Mr. Hooten took the bottle, smacked his lips a few more times and then started to drink. He really *was* thirsty: he drank more than half the bottle before handing it back to Billy.

"That's good stuff," he said, looking around Billy so that he could see the television.

"Movie's pretty good, too," he added, his head

dropping back to the chair. Within seconds, he was snoring, mouth open even wider than before.

Billy carefully set the bottle of water down on the table beside his father's chair and carefully—quietly—backed out of the room.

Standing in the kitchen, Billy sighed with relief. *That was close*, he thought, but it did not deter him from what he was about to do. "Nothing can hold me back now," he whispered, taking a deep breath before reaching for the doorknob.

And stepping out the back door into the night.

The night was cool, the damp, smoky smell of autumn heavy in the air, and Billy stood on his back porch, letting the chilly fall breeze pass over him.

This was it, the moment he'd been waiting for all week. As he leaped down from the steps on his way to hop up and over the wall, he heard a tiny voice call to him.

"Hey, Billy!"

Billy froze midjump, slowly turning in the direction of the little-girl voice. He'd considered attempting to hide in a patch of shadow, but that trick never worked.

She had seen him.

"Hello, Victoria," he said, turning to look up at the second-floor window of the house next door.

The five-year-old had opened the window of her bedroom and was looking down at him in the yard.

"Whatcha doin'?" she asked cheerfully.

As much as he hated to even think about such things, the little girl had an extreme crush on him, and often wanted to hang around when he was doing important things—like building a robot. Billy strongly believed it was the five-year-old's bothersome ways that prevented him from achieving his glory.

"Stuff," he answered, annoyed that she was keeping him from his mission. But he could never be too careful with Victoria Grace McDevitt. All he needed was for her to alert her parents to his being in the backyard and his adventure would end before it even started.

It was easier to play the kindergartner's game.

"What kind of stuff?" She tilted her head like a curious puppy, playing with a lock of her curly blond hair. He could see that she was dressed in her nightgown and guessed that she should have been asleep already.

"Why aren't you asleep?" he asked, hoping to scare her back into bed.

She shrugged.

"Why are you dressed like a superhero?" she asked him.

Billy was startled by the question, looking around the yard just to be sure nobody was around to hear.

"Shhhhh!" he told her, bringing a gloved finger up to his mouth. "It's a secret."

Victoria's eyes bugged from her round face and she smiled mischievously. "Cool," she squeaked. "Can I be a superhero, too?"

He was going to need to be careful with this one, he thought, scratching the top of his head as he tried to come up with an answer that didn't get her all riled up. There was nothing more dangerous than a riled-up five-year-old.

"Not right now," he told her. "But maybe later."

"When?" she demanded.

"I don't know—some other time when it's not so late."

"Tomorrow?"

He really needed to get going and was on the verge of losing his patience with the little girl.

"Yeah, tomorrow you can be a superhero, too."

"Hurray!" Victoria squealed, throwing her tiny arms into the air. "Me and Billy are going to be superheroes tomorrow!" She started to pretend that she was flying around her room, making a racket that was sure to attract the attention of her folks.

"Victoria, knock it off!" he called up to her. "If you want to be a superhero with me, you've got to get plenty of rest."

She stopped pretending to fly and looked down at him.

"Why?"

"Because if you're too tired, how are you going to beat up the bad guys?"

She thought about that for a minute.

"Good night, Billy!" she suddenly said, closing the window and disappearing into the room.

He stood there for a moment watching the window, wanting to be sure she wasn't going to come back. Once he was certain she'd actually gone to bed, he ran toward the stone wall, desperate to get out of the yard and into the cemetery before something else came up to keep him from his destination.

The journey to the mausoleum went off without a hitch. With not a moment's hesitation, Billy pushed the heavy metal door of the burial chamber open and went inside the crypt. He looked around the room through the goggles' special lenses, searching for any signs of the unusual, but found nothing.

He walked to the back of the room, to the stone coffin with the heavy lid still slightly ajar. Unzipping the front of his jumpsuit, he reached inside the costume, searching for something important he had hidden there before leaving his bedroom.

"There you are," he said, producing the owl-shaped whistle. He approached the stone coffin again, but not too close, remembering the last time he had been there.

He hoped to enter Monstros City a little less spectacularly this time.

He put the whistle to his mouth and gave it a forceful blow. The chamber was filled with the sound of hundreds of hooting owls, and Billy felt a wave of goose bumps—*they probably should be owl bumps*—spread across his arms, neck and back.

Just like before, Billy listened to the wind outside the mausoleum pick up, rattling what was left of the leaves in the trees and moaning like a restless spirit.

He looked toward the open coffin, waiting for Archebold to arrive . . . and waited and waited and waited. The goblin didn't come. Billy was starting to get a bit worried, wondering whether he had taken too long to make his decision to be Owlboy. *Maybe he's already found somebody else?* he thought, his brain in a tizzy. He started to panic. *Maybe Archebold saw me in the costume and thought I looked stupid.*

Maybe he had blown his chance to be a real live superhero.

Billy felt himself on the way to being completely depressed, and thought about blowing the whistle again . . . but what was the use?

Not feeling much like a superhero at that moment, more like a superloser, Billy considered his options. He *could* jump down into the coffin and go to

Monstros on his own, but that didn't seem to be the smartest idea. Something told him that Monstros could be a very dangerous place, superhero or not. Or he could just go home, take the costume off, throw it into the back of the closet and never think of this crazy business again.

He knew the safest answer, but he wasn't sure that *safe* was what he wanted.

Looking at the coffin again, he hoped for something to change his mind, but it didn't appear. Knowing then without a doubt that he had been replaced, Billy wished whoever had been chosen for the Owlboy job over him good luck and slowly turned away from the entrance to Monstros City, ready to head home.

At first it sounded like the wind, leaves whipping around, rustling on the ground, carrying over from when he'd first blown the whistle, but then he realized that the sound was coming from behind him.

Almost at the door to leave, Billy turned toward the stone coffin, watching as two tiny hands appeared and Archebold hauled himself up over the edge.

"You came!" Billy cried, barely able to contain his excitement. "It's about stinkin' time!"

"Sorry I'm late," the goblin said, brushing dirt and dust from the front of his tuxedo suit. "Looks like you're in for a busy night."

Archebold then looked at Billy, his small, animal-like yellow eyes glowing in the darkness of the chamber.

"Are you ready for this, Billy Hooten?" the goblin asked.

Billy felt his legs begin to wobble and thought they might just start acting on their own, running with the rest of his body in tow out the door, but he made them obey.

"Yes," he said, nodding eagerly, the dream where he'd been turned into a sandwich suddenly replaying like a summer rerun inside his head before he wished it away.

"Then what are we waiting for?" Archebold asked, motioning with his hand for Billy to follow him as he dove back into the darkness of the coffin.

Billy followed, keeping his fingers crossed that Monstros City wasn't one of those places where dreams really did come true.

CHAPTER 8

"Watch your step," Archebold said from in front of Billy on the curving, shadow steps.

"Believe me, I know," Billy said, on the verge of activating the night-vision goggles covering his glasses. He didn't want a replay of the last time he'd visited Monstros.

Archebold stopped short, turning toward him on the step below. "You know?" the goblin asked him. "How would you know unless . . ."

Billy started to explain, not wanting to get into trouble with the little guy.

"Well, I was going to give your costume back, and I blew the whistle, and along came this wind, which made me lose my balance and . . ."

"So it was you that stopped that robbery that the Monstros newspapers are all buzzing about?"

"The newspapers are buzzing?" Billy asked excitedly. "About me?"

Archebold stroked his chin, a smile on his homely face. "They certainly are," he answered. "That was a great piece of publicity—good thinking."

"But I didn't do it on purpose," Billy tried to explain as the goblin continued to descend. "I was just—"

"We're getting to the really dark part here," Archebold said, coming to a stop. "Give me a second and I'll find us a little light so we don't fall and break our heads." He started to rummage through the inside pockets of his jacket. "I thought I brought him with me. . . . Ah! There you are."

Archebold pulled something large from inside his coat, giving it a good shake.

"Wake up!" the goblin yelled, and suddenly the stairway was illuminated by a bright yellow light.

"What the heck is that?" Billy asked, shielding his eyes from the glow.

"It's just Walter," Archebold said.

Walter was the biggest firefly Billy had ever seen in his life.

"Just Walter," the bug mimicked, wings fluttering as he hovered in the air before them. "Perhaps if I should turn off my glowing posterior, I could perhaps receive a little more respect, hmmm?"

"Oh my gosh, it talks!" Billy said, shocked.

The bug glared at him, and Billy saw multiple representations of himself in his full superhero attire reflected in the bug's bulbous compound eyes.

"Are you sure about this one, Archebold?" the bug asked. "He doesn't seem all that bright."

"Nothing to concern yourself with there, Walter," Archebold told the bug. "You just worry about lighting the stairs so we don't fall and kill ourselves."

"You're the boss," Walter said, flying ahead a bit to light their descent.

"I didn't mean to insult him," Billy said to Archebold as he followed. "It's just that I've never seen a giant talking firefly before."

The goblin smiled widely, showing off a double row of crazy picket-fence–type teeth. "Just you wait and see, yes, sir," he said. "You ain't seen nothing yet."

They finally arrived at the bottom of the steps and stood within an open area of tunnel that seemed very familiar to Billy.

"This is where I ended up before I went to the grocery and stopped the skeletons," Billy said, following the glowing bug and the goblin.

"Think so?" Archebold asked.

"Well, it looks the same," Billy said.

Archebold chuckled, shaking his large head from side to side. "We're nowhere near there."

"But it looks . . ."

"Where you ended up was way back there." Archebold pointed to a darkened area of the tunnel that looked just like the tunnel they were standing in.

"Oh, I get it," Billy said, humoring the goblin.

"I know you can't see it now, but a few more visits and you'll see the difference," the goblin explained. "These shadow tunnels can be sort of tricky. C'mon, where we're going is right up here."

They came to a stop in front of a door that didn't look much different from the door that had taken him into the back room of the monster grocery store, but this time Billy kept the observation to himself.

"Are we done?" Walter the firefly asked as he hovered in front of the door.

"Yeah, that just about does it," Archebold told him. The goblin then opened his jacket, plucking the large bug from the air.

"Good luck with *that* one," the bug said before going into the goblin's coat pocket, its large eyes looking at Billy and then back at Archebold. "Did I mention that I don't think he's all that bright?"

"Don't you worry about it, Walt," Archebold told

him, shoving the bug deep inside the pocket. "I've got everything under control."

The goblin looked back at Billy, rubbing his hands together eagerly. "Are you ready?" he asked.

"I-I-I think so," Billy stammered, the firefly's words damaging his confidence just a little.

"Aw, don't listen to him," Archebold said, reaching into another pocket of his tuxedo and searching for something. "He didn't think the last Owlboy was any good either."

Archebold pulled a large gold key from the pocket and presented it to Billy.

"Here ya go," he said. "I'll let you do the honors."

It was an old-fashioned key like some that Billy had seen at his grandfather's house, only this one was much larger, with the head of an owl at the end.

Billy put the key inside the keyhole and gave it a turn. There was a loud clicking sound as it went in, and then a clacking as he turned it sharply to the right.

The door creaked slowly open, and Billy stepped inside the room, holding his breath, wondering what strange sight could be waiting for him on the other side.

And strange it was.

The room was big, its ceiling rounded, and everywhere he looked there were televisions in all shapes and sizes, old as well as new, stacked up against the curved walls. Each one seemed to be tuned to a different channel, and as Billy looked closer, he guessed that these were views from all over Monstros City. There was also a reclining chair, just like the one his dad had, in the center of the room.

"Where are we?" Billy asked in awe.

"This is the monitoring room," Archebold explained, taking the key from the door and returning it to his pocket. "The part of the Roost where he keeps a watchful eye on Monstros."

Billy quickly looked away from the screens and the varying images of what was going on all over the amazing city to look at the goblin.

"Did you say the Roost?" he asked.

Archebold nodded. "I certainly did."

"As in Owlboy's secret hideout?"

The goblin nodded again. "Yep, a place you can come and hang out and invent stuff to help with your crime-fighting—when you're not out righting wrongs and thwarting evil, that is."

Billy had always wanted a secret hideout but knew there was zero chance of keeping it secret from his parents, or from Victoria next door. This was just too awesome for words.

"My very own secret hideout," he said, barely able to contain his excitement.

"Well, not quite yours yet," Archebold said, shaking a chubby clawed finger at him.

Billy looked at him with dismay. "What do you mean? I thought—?"

"First we have to see if you're ready," the goblin explained, rubbing his hands together in anticipation.

"First you've got to complete Owlboy training."

Again Billy found himself someplace dark.

After leaving the monitoring room, Archebold had escorted him down a long, winding hallway, past a multitude of doors, each of them with a little sign telling what was inside: SCIENCE ROOM, COSTUME ROOM, MUSIC ROOM, VEHICLE ROOM, there was even a SNACK ROOM, and Billy couldn't wait to check out each and every one of them.

But first there was training. *Whatever the heck that means.*

The goblin shoved him through a door which said TRAINING ROOM on it. Left standing in the dark, Billy was starting to get a little anxious, when he heard Archebold's voice.

"All righty then," the goblin said. It sounded as if he were talking through an old loudspeaker. "Let's get this show on the road, shall we?"

Billy looked around, trying to pinpoint where in the room the voice was coming from.

"Where are you?" he asked the darkness, just as the lights came on.

"Holy crap!" Billy exclaimed, using a word his mother despised. She would much rather he use *poop* in his exclamations, but that just sounded stupid.

Billy was standing in a giant room made up to look like a city street. It pretty much looked like any street he'd seen before, with its buildings and shops, but he knew otherwise. This wasn't just your average city street—this was a *Monstros City* street.

"I'm up here, Billy," he heard Archebold say through the crackling speaker, and he looked up to see the goblin waving to him from a booth high up near the ceiling. He was sitting behind what looked like a large panel of controls. *Controls for what?* Billy wondered.

"This is where I'll be conducting your exam," Archebold said, speaking into a large microphone.

"An exam?" Billy nervously yelled up to the goblin. "But I didn't bring a pencil."

"Don't worry," Archebold said, cracking the knuckles of his tiny hands before they started to move around the control panel, pushing buttons and turning cranks. "It's not a written exam."

Billy sighed with relief. He hated written exams, especially ones he hadn't studied for.

"This exam has a much more physical nature."

"Physical?" Billy asked, his apprehension on the rise.

"This test will show me how ready you are to take on the title of Owlboy." The goblin appeared very busy up in the booth, moving around in a flurry of activity.

"It's called Save the Citizens, and it'll show me everything I need to know," Archebold said.

Billy looked around at the fake city streets. "But there aren't any," he said, feeling confused. "Citizens, I mean."

Suddenly, the air was filled with the sounds of whirring machinery. Hatches opened up in the floor, ejecting dummies.

"Here they are," the goblin said.

If Billy hadn't known before, he certainly knew then. After looking at the dummies, there was no way he could've been any place other than Monstros City. These weren't the average dummies that you'd see in department stores of men, women and kids; these were dummies of creatures—*monsters*—of all shapes and sizes. Billy saw wolf-men, giant bugs and a fat old lady with snakes for hair who was pushing a shopping cart.

"So I'm supposed to save them?" he called to Archebold in the control booth.

"That would be a yes," the goblin said, flicking some more switches and causing the lights inside the chamber to momentarily flicker.

"And I'm supposed to be saving them from . . . ?"

Billy asked, looking around the artificial street for any signs of danger. "Doesn't look like there's anything too dangerous around here."

That was when Archebold started to laugh, a creepy sound that didn't make Billy feel all that comfortable.

"I'll show you dangerous," the goblin said, chuckling. He reached inside his coat pocket and removed a hat, slipping it onto his large head. Billy adjusted the mechanisms on his goggles to find the telephoto lens and read what it said on the front of the black ball cap.

#1 Villain! was stitched in red across the front of the cap. Billy found himself growing increasingly nervous.

The goblin flipped more switches, and the large room was filled with the sound of machinery.

Billy turned toward the noise and saw that a brick wall directly across from him had fallen away to reveal what looked like some kind of weapon.

"What the heck?" he exclaimed, watching as the weapon's long silver barrel emerged from its hiding place.

"It's a cannon," he said with growing horror, watching as it took aim at the gathered dummies.

"Save 'em, Owlboy!" Archebold cried, his voice echoing in the training chamber. "If you can."

The cannon fired with a thunderous explosion of compressed air, and Billy was shocked to see a gigantic red ball, instead of some explosive projectile, erupt from the barrel of the huge gun. The ball missed the dummies, bouncing off a building wall and coming at him at incredible speed. He dove out of its path just in time for the ball to rebound off the front of a fake apartment building behind him, ricochet around the room and finally come to a rolling stop nearby.

And then it hit him like an ice cream brain freeze. *The gun is firing dodgeballs*, he realized. *Bigger and faster than the ones thrown by Killer Kulkowski.*

Even here in Monstros he couldn't avoid the stupid game.

The cannon took aim again. Billy jumped toward the weapon, surprised again by the distance he was able to cover in just one leap. The rules were different in Monstros City, he reminded himself, landing in a crouch in front of the gathering of dummies just as the cannon shot another ball.

F'THOOM!

He used the memory of how he'd been the last guy standing in the dodgeball game the other day, and how he had stood up against Killer Kulkowski, to psych himself up as he sprang into the path of the hurtling ball, catching it against his chest.

Or at least that was what he attempted to do.

The ball hit him like a giant fist, lifting him off his feet, almost knocking one of his rubber boots off, and sending him hurtling backward into the dummies. The fake citizens went flying.

"Watch out for the innocent bystanders," Archebold scolded over the speakers. "With heroes like you, who needs villains?"

"I'll give you an innocent bystander," Billy grumbled, allowing the large ball to roll away from him as he got to his feet. It felt as though he'd just been punched in the chest by the entire sixth grade, and by the looks of it, the weapon was getting ready to fire again.

"Jeez, gimme a break," he said, pushing himself to get moving again.

This time I'll take care of the citizens, he thought, and with a show of unbelievable might started to pick up the monster figures one at a time and stack them over his shoulder. It appeared that being in Monstros had given him a boost in strength as well. He had just about collected all the dummy bystanders when the weapon discharged. Carefully balancing the fake citizens on his shoulder, he turned to see where the ball was going and was struck from behind. He and all those he had attempted to rescue went tumbling into a heap.

"Oh!" Archebold screeched excitedly from the booth. "Score one for the bad guys!"

Temporarily trapped beneath the pile of dummies, Billy emerged feeling madder than he had in quite a while, the last such incident having something to do with an atomic wedgie and being hung from a doorknob.

It hadn't been one of his finer moments, and neither was this.

"Whatcha gonna do . . . Owlboy?" Archebold teased, his squeaky voice over the speaker system only making Billy angrier.

"I'll show you what I'm gonna do," Billy blurted, adjusting the goggles on his face before marching toward the cannon. He had a plan. It was a little bit crazy, but at this point it was all he had.

"Oh no you don't!" Archebold said, and Billy could see the goblin in the booth above quickly manipulating the controls to aim the cannon directly at him.

Billy had noticed a whirring sound before the big gun fired, and he was hearing the sound right at that very moment. Standing in the path of the dodgeball cannon, he jumped up as it was about to fire. He grabbed hold of the thick silver barrel. Using every bit of his newfound superstrength, he bent the metal muzzle toward the ceiling and, with a loud grunt of exertion, pinched the end of the cannon off.

"Try shooting me now," he said, a little out of breath as he dropped down to the floor, curious to see if his plan had worked.

The gun tried to fire, but it wasn't successful. Billy dove for cover, suspecting what was going to happen as the weapon suddenly rumbled, shook and then exploded, sending thick black smoke, twisted metal and hundreds of flying dodgeballs into the air.

Billy peeked out from behind the cover of the fat lady with the snakes for hair and her shopping cart, and as the smoke started to clear, he saw the full effect of his maneuver.

"Did I do that?" he asked as the bouncing balls started to settle and he saw what little was left of the dodgeball cannon. He couldn't help looking up at the control booth and smiling.

Archebold was standing in the window of the booth, a look of absolute shock upon his face.

"You . . . you broke the bombardment gun," he stated in disbelief.

Billy looked over at the smoking remains of the weapon. "Yeah, sorry about that. I guess I was madder than I thought." He made a muscle, feeling it through the material of his costume. It didn't pack much of a wallop back home, but here . . .

Archebold pulled his #1 Villain cap down tighter on his gourd-shaped head and returned his attention to the controls in front of him.

"No problem," the goblin muttered as he flicked

some more switches. "I'll just get Halifax to fix it later. Let's pump up the volume a bit, shall we?"

Billy was about to ask who, or what, a Halifax was, but he never got the opportunity. The floor rumbled beneath his feet, and he watched as a section of artificial building pulled apart like two puzzle pieces to reveal one of the craziest-looking contraptions he had ever seen. It looked like a giant pair of robot legs. At the end of the legs was an equally gigantic pair of feet. But the weirdest part—*as if it could get any weirder*—was that the feet were wearing giant sneakers.

A creature covered in thick brownish fur and wearing dirty, grease-stained overalls was sitting in a high-backed seat between the mechanical legs, operating them with a series of levers. He gave Billy a little wave.

"What the heck is that?" Billy yelled up to the goblin with a chuckle, but just as the question had left his mouth, he watched in horror as the giant feet began stomping their way right toward the pile of dummy citizens he was supposed to be protecting.

"Remember the object of the game," Archebold called out in an annoying singsong voice. "Oh, dear me, it looks like those poor people are about to get squashed."

If he wanted to go through with this—if he *really* wanted to be Owlboy—Billy knew he had to do something quickly. His thoughts racing, he ran toward the dummies, trying to come up with the best way to get them out of the path of the mechanical stomping feet.

And then he saw it.

Yahtzee! Billy dove for the shopping cart of the lady with the snakes for hair.

Really putting on the speed, he righted the tipped cart and wheeled it toward the dummies.

The feet were coming closer, and he could feel the vibrating footfalls through the floor as he managed to pick up each and every dummy and load it into the cart.

After moving the last of the citizens—a werewolf wearing sunglasses, with a pink bow in her hair—Billy rushed to push the cart toward the center of the street. Seconds after he'd left the spot, one of the giant mechanical sneakers came down, missing him by a hair.

"Hey, that was kinda close!" Billy yelled up to the furry beast.

"Not close enough," the creature growled, and the legs lurched toward him, ready to stomp him and the dummies to paste.

Billy started to run with the cart, turning his head to see if the feet were keeping up. Surprisingly, they were. In fact, they picked up speed and started to jog. Putting everything he had into it, Billy managed to get ahead of his pursuer, but he knew it wouldn't be for long.

He was beginning to realize that running wasn't the answer. Putting his brain cells into overdrive, he came up with another idea.

He wheeled the cartful of citizens onto the fake sidewalk beside the front steps of an apartment building. He removed the dummies from the cart and sat them on the apartment steps, an audience for what he hoped would follow.

"Now, if you'll excuse me, folks, I've got some things I need to take care of."

Along the street he found the dodgeballs that had been scattered by the explosion of the bombardment cannon and started to gather them in the now empty cart.

"What's that, Billy?" Archebold asked. "Cleaning up before you're defeated by my stomping feet of doom? How nice."

And then the goblin started to laugh maniacally.

Archebold really seems to be getting into this whole supervillain thing, Billy thought as he collected the last of the big red rubber balls.

He backed away from the cart and looked down the street at the mechanical feet. The legs had come to a stop, the hairy driver watching him from within a forest of fur.

"C'mon," Billy urged, striding closer. "I'm waiting for you."

He'd presented himself as bait, but the driver of

the feet and legs wasn't biting. This called for drastic measures.

"Don't you want to stomp me? Well, here I am." Billy watched him, waiting for a reaction, but still there was nothing.

It was time to pull out the big guns.

"What's the matter? Are you afraid . . . *Mary?*"

Being called by a girl's name—especially Mary, for some reason—was the ultimate attack on somebody's courage. It was always guaranteed—well, at least at Connery Elementary School—to get an explosive reaction.

Billy guessed correctly that the reaction would be similar here in Monstros.

"*Mary!*" he heard the hairy driver exclaim. "I'll show you who's a Mary!"

The mechanical legs started toward him, stomping the ground so hard that huge cracks appeared in the blacktop.

For a moment, Billy felt what could have been a touch of fear in the pit of his belly. Then he realized that it could also be the General Tso's Chicken he'd had that night.

Did the other Owlboys feel fear when facing the diabolical inventions of Dr. Mechano or the giant crabs of Sygnis 7? he wondered.

Never.

So it had to be the chicken.

The sneaker-wearing mechanical feet were almost upon him. Billy knew it was time. As the device bore down on him and a foot rose up to squash him flat, Billy tipped over the cart of dodgeballs.

Leaping from the path of the foot's descent, Billy rolled onto his stomach to see if his latest scheme had worked. Coming down on top of the balls, the mechanical leg lost its balance. Billy could see the hairy driver attempting to regain the leg's footing, but no matter where the giant sneakers fell, they landed on rubber balls. Unable to stabilize itself, the device tipped dangerously to one side, crashing through the front of one of the fake apartment buildings.

"Yes!" Billy cheered, his fist shooting up into the air in victory. He watched with interest as the overall-wearing creature emerged from the rubble of the demolished building, jumped down from the wreckage of his craft and ran up the street.

"I've had enough of this!" he cried out, disappearing through a doorway into one of the fake stores.

"You'd better run," Billy called after him. "Teach you to fool around with Owlboy."

For the first time, the name felt right coming out of his mouth.

But his victory was short-lived.

"Not so fast, Hooten," Archebold called. "I'm not done with you yet, I'm sorry to say."

Billy tensed, wondering where the next threat to him—and the dummy citizens—would be coming from.

Suddenly, a spotlight blazed to life and illuminated an area not far ahead. Billy could see what looked like a kind of finish line. A white sign spelled out SAFETY ZONE in big red letters.

"You still have to get those under your protection to safety," Archebold said. "Do you think you can handle that?"

Billy knew it wasn't likely to be easy. Archebold—at least this version of Archebold, doing his best imitation of a supervillain—was sure to have some tricks up his tuxedo sleeve.

"Handle it?" Billy said with all the confidence he could find. "I'm just getting warmed up."

With those words, he dashed to the steps of the apartment building, retrieving the dummies and again placing them inside the shopping cart.

He didn't wait to see what the goblin had in store for him, grabbing hold of the handle of the cart and starting to push toward the finish line.

"Please keep your hands, feet and tentacles inside the cart until it comes to a complete stop," he said as he began to pick up speed.

Archebold's laugh echoed throughout the structure, and Billy braced himself.

A hidden hatch in the ground ahead suddenly slid back and a long mechanical arm with twin spinning buzz-saw blades emerged, blocking his path. Billy barely had a chance to react. Pure instinct kicked in.

This is what it must feel like, he thought, as he sank the heels of his rubber boots into the street, bringing the grocery cart to a sudden stop. *What it feels like to be a hero.*

No chance getting by those, he observed. The spinning buzz-saw blades blocked his way to the safety zone.

Billy had no choice and squatted down, grunting with exertion as he picked up the full shopping cart in his arms.

"If I can't get past them, I'll just have to go over them," he said, and started to run full-tilt toward the spinning blades.

"Have you lost your mind, Billy?" Archebold asked mockingly, still in his supervillain mode. "The blades will cut you and those under your care into bacon!"

Billy thought he knew what he was doing, running as fast as he could toward the newest deathtrap, being extra careful not to spill the citizens from the cart. He was going to need to time this just right.

Just as the spinning blades were being thrust at him

at the ends of their mechanical arms, Billy jumped with all his strength.

Even with the additional weight of the cart, he soared over the revolving blades, landing in a stumbling run. The safety zone was even closer now, and he dropped the cart back on its rubber wheels and began pushing it toward victory.

"Impressive," Archebold growled. "But you're not out of the woods yet!"

Billy pushed the shopping cart all the faster, victory so close that he could practically taste it.

And what does victory taste like? he pondered, feeling his heart beating in his chest so hard that he was afraid it might break through his ribs and fall onto the street. *Probably like a double-thick chocolate milk shake with extra whipped cream and free refills.*

And then he heard the weird buzzing sound. *This can't be anything good.* Billy didn't want to slow down, but curiosity got the better of him and he turned away from the looming finish line.

At first he thought it was a swarm of bees, but as they got closer, he saw that it was worse.

Much worse.

He guessed they must have been some kind of winged fairies—about three inches high—and there was a whole swarm of them gaining on him pretty quickly. Within seconds, they were buzzing around his head, an angry cloud that practically blinded him with its assault.

Billy waved his arms around, trying to disperse the nasty creatures.

"Get out of here!" he screamed. "Can't you see I'm wicked close to winning this?" He continued to swat the air, and then he felt the first sting.

"Yeeowch!" he cried. It was a sharp pain in the side of his neck, and his hand immediately shot to the area.

"That hurt," he said angrily to the tiny creatures buzzing around his face.

The nasty fairies all started to laugh, and he saw that each of them held an elastic band.

"You cut that out!" Billy warned, squinting through his goggles as the fairies started to fire. Even through his costume, the elastics hurt. Billy yelped as he was struck again and again.

"Quit it!" he cried, swatting at his attackers.

The fairies laughed harder. They had formed a large buzzing cloud in the air in front of him, forcing him back from the cart.

Over the annoying buzz of his tiny opponents, Billy thought he heard a strange grinding sound and looked out from behind his hands. The ground in front of his shopping cart was sliding apart to reveal a bubbling pit of molten lava.

"This hero business doesn't get any easier," he muttered, trying to fight his way toward the cart, but the fairies let even more eleastic bands fly, driving him back.

"You were so close," Archebold mocked. "But close doesn't cut it when you want to be Owlboy. Too many are depending on you for you to be second best."

"I'm not second best!" Billy yelled, his body stinging from each new elastic strike. "I almost did it!"

"But almost isn't good enough, is it, Billy?" the goblin asked. "Almost doesn't make you Owlboy."

Billy lowered his hands to fix his gaze on the tiny attackers.

"No, it doesn't," he said.

The fairies were pulling back on the latest volley of elastic bands as the shopping cart slowly started to roll toward the open pit. They were clumped in the air together, their insect wings fluttering so fast that they were practically invisible.

Take them out of the air—problem solved, Billy thought, reaching up to fumble at his throat and undoing the clasp that held his cape on.

Before the fairies could figure out what he was doing, Billy had removed his cape and thrown it over the flying mass. The fairies fell to the street, weighted down by the cape, screaming out in panic.

Billy was proud of his quick thinking, but there was no time for congratulations. The shopping cart full of citizens was teetering at the edge of the opening in the street, about to plunge into the molten lava.

Billy dove at the cart, catching one of the rubber wheels and yanking it away from the edge just as it was about to spill over. Then he picked up the cart again and sprinted toward the safety zone.

Billy didn't know what to expect. He half suspected that Archebold would have something else equally dangerous waiting for him there. But he passed beneath the finish line with no further problems, dropping the cart to the ground and falling to his knees as he breathed a sigh of relief.

Panting like a tired dog on a hot summer's day, Billy suddenly heard the sound of clapping. He looked up to see a smiling Archebold strolling toward him.

"Good job," the goblin said, removing the #1 Villain hat and tossing it aside. "I knew you could do it."

"So what now?" Billy asked, gulping mouthfuls of air. "More tests?"

Archebold turned, marching off toward an open doorway. "We're done with tests," he said, turning around with a grin and a twinkle in his beady eyes as he was about to leave the room.

"Now it's time for snacks."

＊ ＊ ＊

Billy sat in the snack room, waiting.

It was a nice room, painted a light shade of blue, the walls covered with framed portraits of the various Owlboys throughout the years. If Billy wasn't mistaken, each of them was holding a plate displaying a dessert.

He got up from his chair for a closer look.

Archebold had brought him to the room right after his Owlboy exam, telling him to relax and that he'd be back with some refreshments. Looking more closely at the items on the portrait plates, Billy wasn't sure if he was all that interested in what passed for snacks in Monstros City.

Is that piece of pie covered in furry red mold? he asked himself, stepping closer to one of the portraits and squinting behind his glasses and goggles.

"Through the ages, the various Owlboys had one thing in common. They all loved their snacks," Archebold said, entering the room holding a serving tray loaded with all kinds of stuff. "From what I understand, that particular Owlboy loved his bloodberry pie."

"Bloodberry pie?" Billy said, wrinkling his nose with disgust. "That doesn't sound too appetizing."

"No," Archebold said, setting the tray down on a table positioned between the room's two seats. "It really isn't. Give me hecklefruit pie any day."

153

The goblin pointed to a particular dessert on a plate. It looked sort of like a piece of apple pie, but there was an odd color about it, as if it had gone bad.

"That's hecklefruit?" Billy asked.

Archebold picked up the plate and held it out for him to examine. "Do you want to try a piece?" he asked, eyes wide as he licked his lips.

Billy shook his head. "That's all right, I'll try something else. You can have it."

"Really?" Archebold asked excitedly, grabbing a fork. "I hope it's fresh." He poked the snack with the fork's tines.

"Hey, is that your face or are you minding it for a monkey?" asked a tiny voice.

Billy looked around the room. "Did you hear that?"

"I've seen better heads on a mug of root beer," said the small voice again.

"Hear what?" Archebold asked, casually looking up from his dessert.

"That voice . . . the one insulting you."

"You're so dumb, I bet you think a pigpen is something you write with."

"That," Billy said. "Did you hear it?"

"What, my pie?" Archebold asked, holding up his plate.

"When they were passing out brains, you thought they said pillows and asked for a soft one," said the dessert.

"Your pie . . . your pie is talking?" Billy asked in amazement.

"Of course it's talking," Archebold said happily, using his fork to break off a piece of the dessert and popping it into his mouth. "It's heckleberry."

"You're so dumb, you bought a donut and brought it back 'cause it had a hole in it," Billy heard coming from the inside of the goblin's mouth as he chewed.

Archebold held out what was left of the treat. "Are you sure you don't want to try it?" he asked. "It's fresh."

"You were so ugly when you were born, your mother said, 'What a treasure,' and then your father said, 'Yeah, let's bury it.' "

"No, I think I'll pass," Billy said politely.

"Suit yourself," the goblin said, devouring the last bite of the heckleberry pie, and the room was suddenly much quieter.

"Delicious," Archebold said, smacking his lips and placing the empty plate back on the tray. "Aren't you going to try anything?"

Billy saw what looked like a tray of cookies. "These look harmless enough," he said, reaching for one. "What are they—oatmeal raisin?"

He brought the cookie up to his mouth, ready to take a bite.

"No, cockroach chunk," the goblin said casually,

looking over the tray to see what he was going to have next. "They're usually quite good."

At first Billy eyed the cookie with disgust, then suspicion, but finally he decided that if he was ever going to be the full-fledged hero of Monstros City, he'd better get acquainted with its food. Without further thought, he took a big bite of the cookie and started to chew.

"What do you think?" Archebold asked, helping himself to a handful of candies that looked like tiny eyeballs. "Pretty tasty, eh?"

Billy tried not to taste it, but a tiny crumb tickled the back of his throat, making him cough, and the full flavor of the cookie flooded his mouth.

He was shocked at how good it tasted.

"Not bad," he said, smacking his lips before eagerly taking another bite. "Not bad at all."

Feeling daring, he helped himself to two more cookies and then bravely decided to try some of the other strange treats. He had a little bit of everything: a bite of a demon donut, a taste of devil's food cake made from real devils, and something that looked, and tasted, an awful lot like cotton candy. Archebold explained that it had been spun by some of Monstros City's finest spider-chefs.

Finally, feeling stuffed, Billy sat back in his chair, re-examining the paintings on the wall.

"So these are all the Owlboys who came before me?" he asked.

Archebold wiped his mouth with a napkin before answering. "The first right up until the last," he said.

Looking at the paintings, Billy noticed the changes in the costume design throughout the ages, going from very old-fashioned to not too different from what he was now wearing.

"How did they get to be Owlboy?" he asked, suddenly wondering if they'd gone through a process similar to what he'd endured. "How were they chosen?"

The goblin poured them each a glass of something he called poltergeist potion. It made the glass tremble and skitter across the surface of the table. Billy snatched up the glass before it danced off the edge. The thick steam rising from the warm drink fogged his goggles as he took a sip. It was quite tasty.

"The mantle of Owlboy is passed on from one to the next, and that has been the case going back to the very first Owlboy, who came to Monstros from the shadow passage in the Sprylock mausoleum many, many years ago. But when the last Owlboy disappeared, the title was never passed on, and Monstros was without a protector."

The goblin smiled, starting to tidy up. "Until now."

"You came to the Sprylock mausoleum—to where the first Owlboy came from—hoping to find the next?"

Archebold nodded, stacking the dirty dishes. "Monstros was falling into lawlessness, the bad squeezing the life from the good. My family had served the Owlboys through the ages, and I took it upon myself to find the one who was destined to return Monstros to the way it used to be—when good triumphed over evil."

Billy thought about the day when he'd first heard Archebold's cries for help, and he came to a startling realization.

"That day in the mausoleum—that pig guy—he was trying to stop you from finding the new Owlboy!"

Archebold picked up the tray. "Villainy has been allowed to grow for too long in Monstros. Just the thought of Owlboy's returning fills those who have evil in their hearts with fear. They tried to stop me but failed. This is how it was supposed to be. This was destiny."

It hit Billy like a hundred pounds of dirty laundry. This wasn't some game he could play whenever he was interested; it was much bigger than that. This was about fighting the bad guys and making people feel safe again.

He wondered if he had what it would take.

He was about to ask Archebold what he thought—whether the goblin believed that he could actually do the job—when a loud, hooting alarm filled the air.

Hoot! Hoot! Hoot! Hoot!

"What's that?" Billy asked, looking around for the source of the sound.

Archebold stood stiffly, the tray clutched tightly in his hands.

"It's trouble," he said ominously. "Big trouble."

CHAPTER 9

They returned to the room where Billy had first entered the Roost. The alarm continued to blare as lights flashed like a pinball machine gone wild. Right away Billy noticed that all the monitors seemed to be focused on one area in particular.

"What's going on here?" he asked, walking over to the sets, trying to figure out exactly what he was seeing.

Archebold moved from television to television, adjusting the picture quality on one set before moving on to the next. "Remember, this is where we keep an eye on Monstros," he said distractedly, giving one of the old sets a solid whack on the side to get the picture to stop flipping.

"But all the monitors seem to be looking at one place," Billy observed.

"Exactly," Archebold said, stepping back to join him. "This is where a crime most horrible has been committed."

Billy felt his stomach jump, as if some of the crazy snacks he'd just been eating were trying to come up for a walk.

"What kind of crime most horrible?" he asked, not really wanting to know the answer.

In the corner of the room, a machine that looked to Billy like an old-fashioned typewriter, only bigger and covered in flashing lights, suddenly came to life, keys clacking noisily as something was printed.

Archebold crossed the room, pulling the paper from the machine as it finished printing. The goblin studied the paper, making strange little clucking sounds.

"Murder," he said, showing Billy the paper. The word had been typed out in big black letters on the white sheet over and over again.

"Murder?" Billy squeaked.

"Exactly," Archebold replied, returning to the printer as it spat out another piece of information. "For the last two weeks, Monstros has been plagued with a series of murder-robberies." He studied the printout. "And from the looks of it, we've got another."

The goblin walked toward Billy, reaching out to

hand him the two pieces of paper. Billy recoiled as if he were being handed a rattlesnake.

"No, thanks," Billy said. "I don't think I want anything to do with murder right now."

"And that's where you're wrong," the goblin said, shoving the papers into his hand. "This will provide us with the perfect opportunity to show Monstros City your stuff."

Archebold spun on his heels, marching out of the room. "C'mon, we've got work to do."

"Do you really think I'm ready for murder?" Billy asked, having to run to keep up with the goblin. "Don't you think it might be a little . . . y'know, big for me?"

"Nonsense, you handled yourself like a real pro in the training room," Archebold said. "Murder is just what we're looking for."

"How about a stolen bike . . . or a lost dog?" Billy suggested. "I think I could handle a lost dog."

Archebold spun around and looked him in the goggles. "This will be excellent publicity for you, trust me. And besides, there aren't any dogs in Monstros City. Our pets are a bit more . . . unusual." Turning again, he gestured for Billy to follow. "Let's get going before the clues get cold."

Billy stopped short, watching as Archebold continued down the hall, chattering away. It was one thing to keep a bunch of skeletons from robbing a store, but *murder* was altogether different. It took a moment for the goblin to realize that Billy wasn't with him.

Archebold stopped and turned around again. "What are you waiting for? C'mon."

"I can't," Billy said, shaking his head. "I just can't."

"What do you mean, you can't?" Archebold asked, stomping toward him. "You're Owlboy now, for freak's sake, and it's time to show everybody that you're back."

Billy didn't know how to respond. His brain sputtered and sparked as he tried to come up with a reason for not investigating, other than the fact that he was afraid.

"I can't because . . ." And suddenly, he had it, the perfect excuse. "Because I don't have any of the tools I'll need to solve the case. You can't expect me to go out there without the proper tools. I'd look like an idiot."

"Hrrmmmm," Archebold said, stroking his chin. "You're right."

Billy almost blacked out, he was suddenly so happy. He was just not ready for anything like a murder, and by the time they figured out what he'd need, enough time would have passed for him to . . .

"Halifax!" Archebold yelled.

Again, that name.

"Who's . . . ?"

A section of a hallway wall suddenly lifted up and

the furry, greasy, overall-wearing creature stepped out to stand behind the goblin.

"You bellowed," Halifax said, his voice low and rough.

"Ah, Halifax," Archebold said, spinning around.

"You're the one who was driving the robot legs and feet," Billy said.

"Can't pull the wool over his eyes," Halifax said, nudging Archebold with his elbow. "Walter was right about this one, wasn't he?" he whispered, talking through the corner of his mouth seemingly so only Archebold could hear.

"Forget about Walter," Archebold scolded. "That bug's got a bad attitude. Halifax, Billy; Billy, Halifax."

Billy waved. "Hey."

"Hey back," the furry creature responded.

"Okay, now that we've got that out of the way," Archebold said. "We need some things to solve a murder. Can you help us?"

Halifax removed a pair of glasses from the front pocket of his overalls and placed them on his furry face. Billy hadn't a clue how the creature could see, the glasses were so dirty. Halifax pulled a small crumpled notebook and stubby pencil from another pocket. "Whaddya need?" he asked.

"Oh, well, um, I'm sure it's nothing you have handy," Billy said nervously. "I can go back home and get everything I need."

"Halifax is a troll, great with his hands, thus he's our gadget guy," Archebold said. "If we don't have it, he can build it . . . isn't that right?" He looked at the creature proudly.

"On some occasions, I even amaze myself," Halifax said.

"That's all right," Billy began.

Archebold stamped his foot. "It's not all right. Our clues are going to be stone-cold if we don't act pretty soon."

Not wanting to make Archebold any angrier, Billy quickly rattled off a list of things he thought he remembered from the comics he'd read.

"Can't promise you miracles," Halifax said, walking back to his opening in the wall. "But let me see what I can do."

The door hadn't been closed behind him for more than a second before it opened again and the hairy creature stepped out, his arms filled with equipment.

Billy's jaw hung open in disbelief as Halifax dumped all the items on his list on the floor between them.

"Sorry about the wait, boys," he said, scratching his belly. "Coupla the items I had to special-order."

"Can we go now?" Archebold asked, turning away and continuing down the hallway toward what looked like an elevator.

Billy started to pick up the items the troll had dropped. "Thanks a lot," he said sarcastically.

"My pleasure," Halifax replied, disappearing back into the opening in the wall.

"Are you coming or not?" Archebold asked impatiently as the doors of the elevator slid open.

Billy grabbed up all the stuff in his arms and ran to the end of the hall, careful not to drop anything. The doors started to slide closed as soon as he entered.

"Where are we going?" he asked the goblin.

"You'll see," Archebold said as the elevator quickly began to drop.

That's all I need, Billy thought, feeling the contents of his stomach rising into his throat. *Another reason to throw up.*

"Aren't you gonna put any of that on?" Archebold asked, nodding toward the equipment Billy held in his arms. "That's what the belt is for, you know."

Billy dropped the armload and picked out the thick yellow belt. It reminded him of the belt his dad wore to hold his tools when doing projects around the house. Billy put all the crime-fighting implements in their special places on the belt.

That Halifax is good, he thought. Every item on his list was present and accounted for, as well as some things he hadn't even thought of.

Archebold looked him over, nodding his approval. "The last Owlboy didn't use a belt," he said. "It's a nice touch."

The elevator came to an abrupt stop, and Billy wondered if it was possible to live with his intestines up in his throat. The doors parted, and he was still collecting himself as Archebold bolted from the elevator.

"C'mon, c'mon, the rate we're going, we'll never catch any bad guys."

Billy followed the goblin into yet another large room, making a mental note for whenever he had a free minute to ask Archebold how big the Roost actually was.

This room was strangely empty except for a single large object in the center, covered with a gray tarp.

"What's under that?" Billy asked, his curiosity piqued.

Archebold's goblin face looked very serious. "It's been quite some time since this has been used," he said, laying a hand upon the covered object. "From what my grandpa said, the last Owlboy used to love to take her out on missions every chance he got."

"What is it?" Billy asked in an excited whisper, but he already had an idea what he was about to see.

Archebold gripped the heavy canvas covering and pulled it away to reveal the shiny yellow vehicle underneath.

"Wow!" was all Billy could say as he looked upon the item he had seen only in the pages of comic books.

The Owlmobile.

The artists hadn't done it justice.

It was the coolest car he had ever seen, shaped like an owl's head: the big, two-sectioned windshield looked like eyes, and the hood of the vehicle tapered to a hooked beak. The car was bright yellow, and in the light of the room it seemed to glow.

"Awesome," Billy said, walking around the amazing vehicle, taking it in from every angle. "I bet it's fast."

He placed a gloved hand on the hood, still not believing that he was actually touching the Owlmobile. He couldn't count the times he'd promised himself that someday he'd have a car as cool-looking as this.

Archebold reached into his coat pocket and pulled out a set of keys.

"Would you like to see how fast?" he asked, a twinkle in his dark eyes.

Billy couldn't find words and just nodded like a nut.

"Then let's get going," Archebold said, approaching the driver's-side door.

"Can I drive?" Billy finally asked.

The goblin made a face. "What, are you crazy? You're just a kid."

"Not fair," Billy griped beneath his breath, opening

the passenger-side door and getting inside. "Can be a stupid superhero, but can't drive a stupid car."

"Excuse me," Archebold said, leaning over Billy's lap to get at the glove compartment.

He popped open the compartment and removed what looked like a gigantic garage door opener. Pointing it at the circular windshield, the goblin pushed a big red button, producing a spectacular result.

The entire wall in front of them began to slowly rise.

"Oh, wow," Billy gasped, fumbling with his seat belt as the outside of the Roost was revealed. "It's amazing!" He looked out over the vast view of a nighttime city lit up with thousands and thousands of lights.

"Monstros City," Archebold said, putting the Owl-mobile in drive and gunning it toward the exit. "The most fantastic city in all the world, and any other place beyond that, if you ask me."

Billy leaned forward in his seat as the vehicle left the confines of the Roost's garage. He wanted to get a good look at the place—this city he would be in charge of protecting. The first thing he noticed was the road they were driving on as the car descended from the Roost. Billy turned around in his seat to get a look at where they had been and almost didn't believe his eyes.

"Is that what I think it is?" he asked Archebold.

"All depends on what you think it is," the goblin teased.

The Roost was inside a giant tree—the biggest tree Billy had ever seen. Watching it gradually come into view through the back window, Billy guessed that the tree was at least ten times bigger than the biggest redwood he had seen on vacation with his parents in California a few years back..

This was a *big* tree—the biggest—growing out of the center of a forest of smaller trees that weren't really all that small—just smaller than the biggest tree ever.

"Okay, the Roost is in a giant tree," he said in disbelief, trying to convince himself of what he was seeing.

"Where else would a roost be?" Archebold responded. "And in case you ever get lost, the tree is in the middle of the Wailing Wood."

Turning back in his seat, Billy took notice of the ramp they were traveling down into the city and realized that they were driving within an enormous furrow that had been cut inside one of the great tree's heavy, low-hanging branches.

After all the stuff he had seen since coming to Monstros, this had to be the one thing that would fry his noodle for sure.

But then he got a good look at the city. A **really** good look.

Billy had never seen a city like it. He had been to Boston, and New York a few times, and even Los Angeles once, but none of them could compare to this. If a crazy person was put in charge of building a city, Billy imagined that it might look something like Monstros.

Archebold slowed a bit as they continued down the tree limb's passage, so that Billy could get a good look. Billy stared in amazement at the bizarre skyline. There were all kinds of buildings, and they mostly seemed to be made from the stuff you'd expect: wood, brick, concrete, steel and glass. But then there were the structures that looked as though they could have been made from something that might have, at one time, been alive. One building, glistening white in the light reflecting off the other buildings, looked as if it was made entirely out of bones—bones of every conceivable size and shape. Another building looked as if it could've been sculpted from green Jell-O. Billy could actually see through the gelatinous structure; he watched the people—*monsters?*—moving around inside as they did whatever it was that monsters who work in buildings made of green Jell-O do.

"Is that green Jell-O?" Billy asked, trying to sound casual.

Archebold snickered, shaking his malformed head as he drove. "Green Jell-O," he scoffed. "That's the Amoeba building; it was grown last year."

"You grow your buildings?" Billy asked, amazed.

The goblin looked surprised. "Yeah, some of them. What's the big deal, doesn't everybody?"

Billy didn't answer, leaning back in his seat and letting the wonder of Monstros wash over him like a wave. They were getting closer to street level, and now he could see some of the smaller, more intimate structures, the stores, restaurants and apartment buildings. Everything seemed normal at first glance, but on closer inspection, it wasn't. One building on the right looked like a gigantic clamshell; another beside it Billy could swear was covered in fur. Further on, yet another looked as though it had been chiseled from a block of ice.

At first it all seemed scary and insane. But soon Billy realized that it was no scarier than going to any new place. Really, it was just like visiting any other city for the first time.

This one just happened to be populated by monsters.

"Well, what do you think?" Archebold asked, gazing out the window with a proud look on his face. "Ain't she a beauty?"

"I think I'm gonna like it here," Billy said.

CHAPTER 10

The Owlmobile rounded the corner at Banshee Boulevard, its headlights like two blazing eyes illuminating the street before it.

The car's thick tires slid across the road with a screech as the vehicle continued down the dark and curving side street. Pulling up to a curb, the car came to a sudden stop, its powerful engine revving momentarily before falling silent, the twin headlights winking out.

"Did I park close enough to the curb?" Archebold asked as he opened the driver's-side door.

Billy had climbed out on the other side. "You're good," he assured the goblin. "This ride is sweet," he added, pulling his attention from the cityscape back to the car as his goblin sidekick joined him on the side-walk. "When do I get to drive it?"

"One thing at a time, Billy," the goblin said, adjusting the jacket of his tuxedo. "There'll be plenty of opportunities for you to drive later. Right now our main focus is to let the denizens of Monstros know that you're back. Remember, they've been waiting for this—for you—for an awfully long time."

Archebold removed a monocle from his jacket pocket and placed it over one of his beady little eyes. "Now, let me take a good look at you."

The single piece of circular glass magnified the goblin's bloodshot peeper to gigantically gross-me-out proportions. *I guess it helps him to see better,* Billy figured. Archebold stepped back, motioning with one of his stubby arms for Billy to turn around.

Billy did as he instructed, slowly spinning in a circle for the goblin's inspection.

"Not bad," Archebold said, rubbing his nubby chin. "A little shorter than the usual, but not bad at all."

"Does it make my butt look big?" Billy asked, trying to look over his shoulder at his costumed behind.

"You look fine," the goblin said, quickly turning to leave, his coattails flapping behind him. "Let's go."

Billy followed tentatively. "So, this will be a murder scene?" he asked.

"Exactly," Archebold said, not bothering to slow down or turn around. He waved a stubby finger in the air for effect. "And it's up to Owlboy to set things right."

Billy stopped short. "You want me"—he gulped—"to solve the murder?"

The goblin was already on the other side of the street, moving toward a muffled commotion. "You're the guy in the Owlboy costume, aren't you?" he shouted.

"Yeah, but I have a hard time with word problems—what makes you think I can solve a murder?"

"C'mon, you'll be great."

Billy chased after the little goblin, making sure to look both ways before crossing the street. After some of the things he'd seen in Monstros City, he didn't want to take the chance of getting run over by a dinosaur passing by, or maybe even a UFO.

Billy caught up with Archebold as the goblin was preparing to head down an alley. "I can't do this," Billy said, reaching out with one of his gloved hands to yank on his friend.

Archebold turned. There was a huge crooked smile on his wide, ugly face. "Of course you can," he said with the utmost confidence.

But Billy felt none of the goblin's certainty. "How do you know?" he asked, gazing down the alley at the crowd ahead. "I'm only twelve years old, for Pete's sake."

" 'Cause you've been *chosen*," the goblin said. "You are Owlboy."

Billy felt a little sick to his stomach. "Chosen," he repeated. "I've been chosen. You keep saying that, but what does it really mean?"

Archebold placed a hand on the front of his white shirt. "I've chosen you." He lifted his hand and waved it around in the air. "This place has chosen you. For hundreds of years it has been my family's job to serve the one who has taken on the mantle of Owlboy, and trust me, I'd know if you weren't the one."

He turned away from Billy and started down the alley once again. "And besides, the costume fits you."

"No, it really didn't," Billy protested, still not feeling any better. "I had to make a lot of alterations."

They were closer to the crowd now, and he could hear the strange voices of the monsters that were gathering as they chattered among themselves, clamoring for the sight of something beyond the alley.

"Cryin' shame," said a monster that looked kind of like a praying mantis, only it was wearing a blond wig, a halter top and a miniskirt.

"Just keeps getting worse and worse," another monster replied, this one bright green and resembling a stalk of asparagus with multiple spindly arms and legs. It was eating an ice cream cone covered in what looked like sprinkles—only, the sprinkles Billy knew didn't squirm around all over his ice cream. "I remember when this part of town used to be safe," it continued between eager licks. Its voice was high-pitched, like the screech of a rusty screen door.

Archebold turned to Billy. "Did you hear that?"

"Yeah, but—"

"No more buts," Archebold warned with a shake of his gourd-shaped head. "Monstros needs you." He gazed lovingly at the buildings around them, and then at the gathering of monsters. "*They* need you."

It was as though those words flicked a switch somewhere in Billy's head. At last, he began to understand.

"They need me," he repeated quietly, allowing the words to rattle around inside his skull. He felt a bond with Monstros City then, and with the creatures that lived there. They needed him to be something more than just a sixth-grade kid—something more, even, than what he believed himself to be.

"Billy, hey, are you all right?" Archebold asked.

"I'm fine," Billy said, adjusting the chinstrap on his leather helmet and straightening the goggles that covered his glasses. "But now I have work to do." He tugged on the cuffs of his mother's gardening gloves, wiggling his fingers around for a better fit.

"Very good, sir." Archebold smiled and nodded with approval.

"*Owlboy* has work to do," Billy said again. This time the name sounded not like an insult, but like something more—something important. He liked the way it sounded.

Taking a deep breath, he plunged into the gathering, moving through a sea of monsters, chasing his destiny.

Billy pushed his way through the crowd. Archebold followed close behind, holding on to the end of his cape.

"Please move aside, good citizens," Billy said, careful not to step on anybody's feet, talons or tentacles. "There is evil afoot that requires my immediate attention."

He said the words in his most grown-up voice, and was surprised to find the residents of Monstros City actually doing as he requested.

"Good one, sir," Archebold said from the rear. "Very heroic sounding."

Billy turned to look over his shoulder. "Well, I *have* been practicing," he said.

At last they emerged from the throng out into the open, and Billy felt the eyes of the crowd upon him.

"Who the heck is that?" he heard one of them ask.

"I'm not sure, but he called us good citizens," commented another.

"I think it's Owlboy . . . but it can't be, he disappeared years ago," squeaked yet another.

The monsters continued to mutter among themselves, not sure what to make of the costumed boy.

Billy couldn't believe his eyes as he stood staring at the crime scene. He had to keep reminding himself that here in Monstros City, nothing was beyond the imagination.

Lying in the middle of the alley before him was a dead cockroach, and not just any cockroach. This was the biggest cockroach Billy had ever seen. It was about the size of Sammy Dana's mom's new minivan, and it was lying on its back with its six legs sticking up in the air. To make matters even stranger, the bug was wearing a baseball cap and had a thick handlebar mustache.

"That's the biggest bug I've ever seen," Billy said, mesmerized.

Archebold shrugged. "I keep forgetting you're not from around here."

The Monstros City police force was already milling about the giant insect, inspecting the scene of the crime. Billy was amused to see that there really didn't seem to be much of a difference between the police officers back home in Bradbury and those of Monstros City, other than the obvious multiple heads and limbs.

"What do you think happened to him?" Billy asked Archebold.

"Don't know," the goblin answered. "But it's your job to find out."

Billy experienced that weird sensation all over again—the one that told him he was doing the right thing. The last time he had felt it this strongly was the day he had answered Archebold's cries for help.

He took a deep breath, preparing himself for what he was supposed to do . . . but he wasn't exactly sure what that was. He was about to ask Archebold for some tips when the goblin began pointing at one of the pockets on the tool belt around his waist.

"What?" Billy asked.

"In the pocket," the goblin whispered.

Billy reached down to one of the pockets on the belt and unsnapped it. Inside was a large magnifying glass.

"It's to search for clues," his sidekick said as Billy looked through the thick glass, noticing how much huger everything appeared.

"Cool," Billy said, inching closer to the scene of the crime.

"And where do you think you're going?" asked a voice so deep that it must have started from the toes— if the guy who said it *had* any toes.

Billy gazed up into the dripping face of a tall, slime-covered beast who really didn't seem to have much of a shape at all. His head was sort of round, and through his semitransparent skin Billy could see things floating around inside. *It's like looking into a dirty fish tank,* Billy thought with revulsion. The creature was also wearing multiple pairs of dark-framed glasses over multiple pairs of eyes. A long gray trench coat buttoned to the top covered his bulbous body, which ended in a short tail that wiggled on the ground and left behind a slimy trail, like a snail.

"I—I—I'm going to investigate the scene of the crime," Billy stammered, not sure what pair of eyes he should be looking at.

The creature began to laugh, his entire body undulating and sloshing as he swayed from side to side. It reminded Billy of a balloon filled with too much water, and he wondered if the strange beastie might burst.

"This is Detective Oozea," Archebold whispered in Billy's ear. "Of the Monstros City police force."

"Got it," Billy whispered back, returning his attention to the still-laughing police detective. "So, if you would be so kind as to allow me to look for clues, I would—"

Detective Oozea just laughed all the harder.

Billy looked at Archebold. "What did I say that was so funny?" he asked.

The goblin shrugged. "Couldn't say, but something tells me he isn't taking you seriously."

The detective wiped tears from beneath his multiple sets of glasses. "Thanks, kid," he said, sounding as if he were speaking underwater. "Haven't had that good a laugh since Jimmy the Pinch got his tentacles stuck in a vending machine down on Lycanthrope Lane."

"You're welcome," Billy responded. "I think."

Another strange denizen of Monstros came up alongside the nearly shapeless detective. This one was dressed in the dark blue uniform of the Monstros City police force, and from the number of gold buttons on the front of his coat, Billy guessed he must be somebody official.

"What do we have here?" the new arrival asked.

"Hey, Chief Bloodwart," Oozea said. "Get a load of this." He pointed a fat, dripping appendage at Billy.

Chief Bloodwart looked as though he had been chiseled from stone, his squat, hard body jagged with angles that threatened to puncture his uniform.

"Now would you look at that," he said, the sound of his voice like two pieces of concrete being rubbed together. "I guess they'll let anyone wear the costume these days."

He and Oozea both laughed then, a grating symphony of strange noises that made Billy wince.

"I don't think this is going so well," he said to Archebold. "Maybe if you explained that I was the new Owlboy, they'd—"

183

"Assert yourself," Archebold instructed him in a whisper. "Show a little confidence."

The detective and chief were still yukking it up as Billy cleared his throat. They composed themselves to hear what he had to say.

"If you two fine . . . gentlemen?"

He looked at Archebold for support. " 'Gentlemen' is good," the goblin said, giving him a thumbs-up. "You're on fire."

"If you two fine gentlemen would clear the way," Billy continued, "I can begin my inspection of the scene, and hopefully bring about the apprehension of the perpetrator, or perpetrators, before the trail goes cold."

Oozea and Bloodwart were silent, staring down at him through numerous sets of eyes, and then slowly turned their gazes to each other. They suddenly burst out hysterically, laughing harder than they had before.

"Apprehension of the perpetrator!" Oozea squealed, his gelatinous body quivering like Billy's Aunt Gertrude's famous Christmas pudding.

Bloodwart was bent over, slapping his rock-hard knee repeatedly with an equally hard hand. "Two fine gentlemen—can you stand it?"

Archebold grabbed Billy by the elbow and escorted him past the two laughing policemen. "C'mon," he said, pulling Billy along. "While we've got the chance."

Billy didn't have to wonder about the other police officers at the scene; they were all laughing too, pointing and carrying on as if he were the funniest thing they had ever seen.

"Geez," he said dejectedly. "A guy could really get a complex around this place."

"Don't pay any attention to them," Archebold told him. "They won't be laughing for long. Go ahead," he urged, nudging Billy closer to the body of the large bug. "Show 'em your stuff."

Billy stood before the dead insect, not sure what his next step should be. The problem, he realized, was that even though he was wearing the costume, he was still thinking like Billy Hooten of Bradbury, Massachusetts. He had to start thinking like Owlboy of Monstros City if he entertained any plans of becoming a real live crime-fighting superhero.

What would Owlboy do now? he pondered.

Billy reached around, pulling his very first Owlboy comic from the back pocket of his costume, and started to flip through the pages.

"I'd be searching for clues, of course," he said, closing the comic book and returning it to his pocket. And with a mighty leap that would have made Mr. Pavlis, his muscle-bound gym teacher, green with envy, Billy hopped up onto the stomach of the monstrous insect for a closer look.

"Hmmmmmm, what do we have here?" Billy asked, looking through the lens of the magnifying glass and finding his first clue almost immediately. There were strange swirling indentations pressed into the surface of the roach's body.

"What did you find?" Archebold asked, scrambling up for a better look.

"Some very unusual marks, wouldn't you say?" Billy handed the goblin his magnifier.

"It's almost as if the poor sap has been squashed by something coiled," Archebold observed.

"Multiple somethings, actually," Billy said, taking back his magnifying glass. He touched the marks on the cockroach's shell. "And they're sticky, too." He looked around, hot on the trail of further incriminating evidence.

"What a way to go," Archebold said with a sad shake of his large head. "You'd think that getting squashed would be the least of your worries when you're this big."

Detective Oozea and Chief Bloodwart had stopped laughing and were ambling closer to the scene of the crime.

"Marks?" Oozea questioned. "I didn't notice any marks."

Bloodwart said nothing, watching Billy as he moved about atop the bug.

"Get down off of there at once!" Oozea demanded. "You'll contaminate the evidence. Hey, you, did you hear me?"

"Let him be," Chief Bloodwart ordered.

Billy felt his confidence rise as he continued with his investigation. He glanced over the side of the roach, noticing something littering the ground below. It looked like wrappers of some kind.

"What do we have here?" he asked, leaping down from his perch to the ground. "Hello there, little clue," he said, squatting down and picking up what appeared to be a candy wrapper. "What kind of fascinating things do you have to tell me?"

He brought the wrapper to his nose and sniffed it.

"Grape," he said. "It appears that our perpetrators have a fondness for grape bubble gum."

"I think a flip through the *Book of Creeps* might be in order, sir," the goblin said.

"*Book of Creeps?*" Billy asked, looking up at Archebold, who was still standing atop the body of the giant bug.

"A reference guide to all the nasty beasts that call Monstros their home," the goblin answered, reaching into his inside coat pocket and fumbling around for something. "Quite handy, really, and it's in here someplace," he continued, deciding to check both sides of his coat for good measure. "Ah, here it is," he said excitedly, pulling out an enormous book that couldn't possibly have fit inside his coat pocket. The book was bound in leather and covered with a fine layer of dust and cobwebs. Archebold brushed off its ancient-looking surface and opened it. "Any time you're ready, sir."

Billy stroked his chin with a gloved hand. "If I'm not mistaken," he said with a certain authority, "our culprits will be of a hopping nature." He made bouncing movements with his hands. "They'll travel in packs and have a penchant for penny candy."

Archebold began to leaf furiously through the yellowed pages of the ancient tome.

"Can you stand it?" Oozea boomed. "'A penchant for penny candy.' Ain't that the sweetest thing? *Bwaaahahahahahaha!*"

Bloodwart remained silent.

"Am I warm?" Billy asked his friend, ignoring Detective Oozea's raucous laughter.

Archebold traced a pudgy finger down the length of a page, suddenly coming to a stop. "You're red-hot, sir!" he screeched excitedly. "It sounds like we're talking about a pack of Slovakian Rot-toothed Hopping Monkey Demons," he added, looking up from the book. "Sheer genius, Owlboy."

"A pack of Slovakian Rot-toothed Hopping Monkey Demons, you say?" Chief Bloodwart asked as he shambled closer. "If I'm not mistaken, the Bounder boys were just released from a twelve-year stint in Kruger Prison three nights ago, and they fit your description to a T."

"The Bounder boys," Detective Oozea said, the fluid inside his body turning a darker shade of gross. "They're a terrible lot. We'll need to call in reinforcements if we're to deal with that motley crew."

Billy adjusted his goggles and puffed out his chest. "No need for that, Detective, I'll handle this."

He motioned for Archebold to follow him. "Come along, Archebold." Billy turned from the scene of the crime and headed toward the crowd and the exit from the alley beyond them. "We haven't a moment to lose. Let's find these Bounder boys and put a stop to their reign of terror."

The crowd had begun to clap and whistle as they approached.

"Go get 'em, Owlboy!" somebody cried. "Glad to have you back!"

"It's about time!" cheered another.

The throng parted to let Billy and the goblin through, clapping their flippers, tentacles and claws as the pair passed.

"How was that?" a smiling Billy asked.

"Most excellent, sir," Archebold said, the cheers of Monstros's citizens following them out into the street. "It sent chills up and down my spine."

The monstrous crowd slowly followed them up the alley to the Owlmobile, continuing to cheer, hoot, whistle and growl the whole way.

"You think I should go out and talk to them some more?" Billy asked excitedly from the passenger seat of the car.

Archebold snapped his seat belt into place and put the key in the car's ignition, starting the engine. "Remember, you've got to stay mysterious. Always keep them guessing. And besides, we have more important things to do than giving pep talks to your adoring public."

"What are we doing now?" Billy asked. He was barely able to get his seat belt on before Archebold put the Owlmobile in drive and screeched out of the parking space into the night.

"I can't believe you even have to ask me that," the goblin said. "Billy, Billy, Billy, remember, you're Owlboy now. And what does Owlboy do after he deduces who the perpetrators of a particular villainy are?" The goblin waited for his answer.

"He . . . he goes after the bad guys?" Billy asked.

"Bingo!" Archebold exclaimed.

"So we're going after the Bounder boys?"

"Now you're thinking like an Owlboy."

Billy grinned, rubbing his gloved hands together eagerly. He didn't think the night could get any cooler, but he was wrong.

They continued to drive through the dark, winding streets of the city, and everywhere the yellow owl's-head–shaped vehicle went, monsters—gigantic or tiny, scaled or hairy, winged or multilimbed—let out some kind of cheer as their hero's car passed by them.

It made Billy proud that he had been chosen, and even more determined not to let them down.

"So where are the Bounder boys hiding?" he asked his friend.

Archebold glanced at him quickly and shrugged. "I haven't a clue."

"You don't?"

The goblin shook his head. "Nope, I'm waiting for you to tell me where to go."

"How the heck am I supposed to know?" Billy asked.

"Because you're Owlboy now—you're the boss."

"Oh, yeah," Billy said, startled by the realization. "I guess I am."

He gazed out the side window, watching the scenery of Monstros City whip by. His eyes caught something of interest far off in the distance.

In all the comics he had read, *Owlboy* or any other superhero comic book, the bad guys always seemed to set up their hideouts in abandoned factories or warehouses. Gazing out the window, Billy thought he might have found just such a place.

"Hey," he said, getting Archebold's attention. "Any of those buildings over there abandoned?"

The goblin craned his neck to see. "That's the old factory district," he said. "Not sure, but I guess they could be."

"If that's the case, one of those buildings would make a perfect hangout for our Slovakian Rot-toothed Hopping Monkey Demons—what do you think?" Billy asked.

The goblin smiled. "I think you might be onto something, boss. Why don't you check that info with Halifax back at the Roost?"

Archebold pushed a button on the dashboard and a large panel opened, revealing a tiny television screen and a phone. "Just push the red button and wait a minute," he told Billy.

Billy picked up the receiver and pushed the button. He could hear the phone ringing on the other end.

The small television suddenly crackled to life, and

the image of Halifax wearing a puffy shower cap, his long, dark fur dripping wet, appeared on the screen.

"Hello?" the troll grumbled.

"Hey, Halifax, it's me," Billy said.

"Me who, and this better be good because you got me out of the bathtub," the troll growled.

"You've done it now, Hooten," Archebold scolded, grinning from pointy ear to pointy ear. "There's nothing Halifax treasures more than his bathtime."

"But you told me to!" Billy exclaimed. "He told me to!" he screeched into the receiver.

"If this is a prank call, I'm going to find out who you are and come to your house and—"

"It's me, Halifax," Billy quickly explained. "It's Bil . . . it's Owlboy."

"Oh," Halifax said, calming down right away. "Why didn't you say so? What can I do for you, sir?"

"I'm really sorry about getting you out of the tub. It's just that I need some information that Archebold said you'd be able to find for me."

"And what would that be?" the troll asked him. "The quicker I give you what you require, the faster I can return to my soothing bubbles after a hard night's work."

"You take bubble baths?" Billy asked in disbelief.

"The information, sir?" Halifax pressed, ignoring the bubbly question.

"Oh yeah, sure," Billy said. "I was wondering if any of the buildings down near the factory district might be abandoned."

Halifax scratched the plastic shower cap on top of his head. "This might take me a while," he finally complained. "So I'm afraid I'm gonna have to call you back." Without warning, the tiny television screen went dark.

"He said it might take a while and that he'll call us back," Billy said to Archebold. He was ready to return the phone to its cradle when it started to ring.

Billy pushed the red button, picking up the call as Halifax appeared on the screen again. "Sorry for the wait, sir, but it's just one interruption after another."

"No problem," Billy said. "What did you find?"

"There is indeed an abandoned structure in that vicinity." Halifax read from a printout. "The Stick-It-To-Ya adhesives factory was closed down a little over a year ago."

"A glue factory," Billy said, stroking his chin and attempting to put the pieces together. "That could explain the sticky marks on the victim's body."

Halifax cleared his throat noisily, catching Billy's attention.

"Will that be all, sir?" the troll asked.

Billy nodded. "Yeah, I think that's good. Thanks, Halifax, you can go back to your bubble bath now."

"Your generosity overwhelms me," Halifax muttered under his breath, breaking the connection.

"I don't think he likes me," Billy said, hanging up the phone.

"Join the club," the goblin replied. "He doesn't like anybody."

Archebold brought the Owlmobile to a stop at a red light, the engine humming powerfully beneath the hood. A giant spider wearing multiple pairs of Rollerblades was struggling to get itself safely across the street before the light changed to green.

"I think we need to check out Stick-It-To-Ya adhesives," Billy said, watching the spider's limbs slipping and sliding out from beneath its large, furry body. "What do you think of that?"

"What do I think?" Archebold asked as the light changed and he drove the Owlmobile expertly around the struggling arachnid.

"I think you're getting the hang of this hero business."

CHAPTER 11

Archebold turned off the car's lights and engine just before they reached the abandoned adhesives factory, allowing the Owlmobile to glide silently to a stop before the front gate. He didn't want to draw any attention to the fact that they had arrived.

"Here we are," Archebold said, putting the car in park.

Billy looked out his window at the chained gate and the large, dark factory building beyond it.

"Kind of ominous, isn't it?" Archebold asked.

Billy studied the structure, its multiple windows boarded up, large brick smokestacks reaching up into the moonlit sky.

"It's more than ominous, Archebold," Billy said in a

serious tone. "The factory resembles some kind of nightmarish plant that has grown up from the bowels of the earth."

He looked over to see the goblin smiling.

"What?" Billy asked.

"Very good, sir," Archebold praised him. "I love the whole nightmare plant thing. Very descriptive."

"Did you like that?" Billy asked. "It just seemed to come to me."

They both got out of the car and approached the gate.

A big CLOSED UNTIL FURTHER NOTICE. NO TRESPASS-ING! sign hung by a rusty chain on the front of the entrance.

"Do you think the Bounder boys can read?" Billy asked.

"I'd probably have to say no," Archebold replied. "Evil is not often represented by the sharpest crayons in the box, sir."

"So there's a good chance that the sign didn't keep them away." Billy tensed his legs, preparing for a mighty leap that would allow him to clear the fence and land on the other side. "Let's get in there and show them—"

He felt Archebold's hand on his sleeve.

"Not so fast, sir," Archebold warned.

Billy turned to his friend. "What's wrong?"

The goblin shook his head. "You're not ready yet."

"What do you mean, I'm not ready?" Billy asked, confused. "You've been telling me all night that I'm ready to be Owlboy."

"And you are," Archebold answered. "But you're not ready to go in there." He pointed to the creepy-looking factory. "With *them*, if they're actually inside. Not yet."

"Fine. What do I have to do to get ready, then?"

"So glad you asked." Archebold was already going through the pockets of his tuxedo jacket.

Those are some pretty deep pockets, Billy thought.

"One of the first rules of being Owlboy is to always know what you're up against. Know your enemy, my granddaddy used to say." The goblin removed the large, dusty leather-bound book from his pocket again.

"Let me guess, the *Book of Creeps?*" Billy asked.

"Precisely," Archebold said. "Everything you'll need to know about Slovakian Rot-toothed Hopping Monkey Demons is right here for your perusal."

"So what's it say?"

The goblin opened the book, sending clouds of dust roiling up into the air and making him cough.

"Here," he said, handing Billy the book. "Hold this." He reached into another pocket. This time, he pulled out a full glass of water, draining it in one large gulp.

"Much better," the goblin said, clearing his throat

and returning the empty glass to his pocket. "Look up Slovakian Rot-toothed Hopping Monkey Demons and see what it says."

Billy flipped through the dusty pages, pleased to see that the entries were in alphabetical order. He found the section for the letter S, surprised at how many species of creep began with it, and quickly scanned the page until he found what he was searching for.

"Here we go. 'Slovakian Rot-toothed Hopping Monkey Demons,'" he read aloud.

"What's it say?" Archebold asked.

"It says that this particular type of monkey demon is extremely dangerous. They have a four-skull rating out of five."

"Good to know," Archebold said, pulling a tiny notepad and pencil from the front pocket of his starched white shirt and writing the information down. "Four skulls."

"And that they have an incredible hunger for anything made of sugar," Billy continued.

"Addicted to sugar. Check," said Archebold.

"Oh, this sounds important," Billy said, reading on. "It says here that the most deadly Slovakian Rot-toothed Hopping Monkey Demons ever to exist are . . ."

He stopped short, looking up from the book, the information startling him into silence.

"Bet I know where this is going," Archebold said.

" 'The worst Slovakian Rot-toothed Hopping Monkey Demons ever to exist are the Brothers Bounder. See Bounder Boys for further information,' " Billy read.

Archebold winced. "Ouch. That's not good."

Billy flipped to the front of the book. "Better see what it says about them." He found the entry and suddenly realized he *really* had to pee.

"Bad, huh?" Archebold asked.

"It says that the Bounder boys are the most dangerous of all the Slovakian Rot-toothed Hopping Monkey Demons and have actually won the prestigious Villains of Distinction award four years in a row."

"Impressive," the goblin commented with a nod. "At least they take pride in their work."

Billy continued, " 'The Bounders have held on to their unique place in the annals of villainy due to their invention of the Bounder boots—special footwear of the brothers' own design, equipped with powerful high-tension coils, enhancing the Hopping Monkeys' ability to jump upon and squash their chosen victims.' "

"That explains the marks found on all the victims," Archebold said as Billy nodded in agreement. "Does it say anything else? Anything that might be useful, maybe?"

"Yeah," Billy said, looking up from the *Book of Creeps* and slamming it closed.

"It says approach with caution."

With Archebold riding piggyback, Billy leaped into the air, easily clearing the high metal gate and landing on the factory grounds beyond it.

"Thanks for the lift," the goblin said, dropping to the ground and adjusting his tuxedo.

"Glad to be of service," Billy said. "So what's the story with my superpowers in Monstros?" he asked curiously. "I could never jump like that back home."

"One thing you'll eventually come to understand, Billy, is that Monstros is different. The rules that apply in your world don't apply here."

"Cool," Billy said, already wondering about the full meaning of the goblin's words. But his curiosity would have to wait until he completed his first assignment as Owlboy.

It was pretty dark on the property, and Billy reached up to activate his night-vision goggles.

"I'm gonna have to get me a pair of those," the goblin said, removing a lit candle from one of his bottomless pockets as they moved closer to the darkened factory.

They tried a bunch of doors, which were either chained or just plain locked from the other side. Billy was starting to think that maybe his theory about the Bounders' hideout might be wrong, when they found a door at the back of the factory that looked as though it might have been tampered with.

Billy held his breath as he gripped the doorknob and gave it a try.

The door clicked open. The heavy chemical smell of glue and something else—something *wild*—wafted out to greet them.

"Do you smell that?" Billy asked, wrinkling his nose as he looked back at his goblin sidekick. "It smells sort of like the monkey cages at the Franklin Park Zoo."

"That's the smell of evil," Archebold said, his eyes twinkling in the darkness. "Mixed with a hint of grape."

"It stinks," Billy said, pinching his nose closed with his fingers.

"What do you expect evil to smell like—roses? If it smelled good, it wouldn't be all that evil, now would it?"

"I think evil needs to take a bath," Billy said.

As they entered the factory, a single lightbulb hanging from the ceiling provided a sickly yellow light. They headed down the dingy corridor in search of the Bounder boys and didn't have far to go before they heard voices.

"The sound of evil?" Billy asked Archebold in a whisper.

"In stereo," the goblin answered softly.

They cautiously continued down the hallway in the direction of the voices.

At the end of the corridor, the room opened up onto the factory floor, and Billy held back, peeking around the corner.

Archebold tugged on his cape, and Billy turned to see the goblin looking up. Billy did the same and spotted a catwalk that extended to the other side of the factory.

Billy gave Archebold a thumbs-up, and they went in search of a way onto the catwalk. They found a ladder, then climbed up to the aerial walkway. The catwalk gave them a perfect view of the entire factory floor, as well as of whoever was speaking.

There were other noises too, wet, gross, smacking sounds that reminded Billy of Randy Kulkowski gorging himself on all-you-can-eat Sloppy Joe day in the school cafeteria.

Squatting at the edge of the catwalk with Archebold right beside him, Billy stared down at the sight of five Slovakian Rot-toothed Hopping Monkey Demons sitting around a makeshift table that had been put together from an old door and an old, rusty metal drum.

The tabletop was covered in their ill-gotten gains, an enormous pile of individually wrapped pieces of candy.

Billy felt a thrill of excitement pass through his body as he observed the creatures going over their sweet bounty. His instincts had been right, and he found himself feeling even more like the costumed hero whom he had come to admire.

"Are you sure you haven't done this whole superhero business before?" Archebold asked with a proud smile.

Billy grinned, feeling ten feet tall, but was quickly beamed back to earth when he realized that he actually had to figure out how to bring these nasty creatures to justice. That would take some careful thought and observation, he decided, peering over the edge of the catwalk and watching the foul beasties in their unnatural habitat. If he had learned one thing from reading all those Owlboy comics, it was how important observing could be.

The Bounder boys were a disgusting bunch, clothed only in bright red vests and deadly-looking coiled shoes. Strangely enough, they were also wearing nametags pinned to their colorful vests, making it much easier for Billy to keep track of who everybody was.

He'd never expected evil to be quite so helpful.

The Bounder boys were arguing.

"You've had enough!" Benny Bounder screeched to his brother, who was busily unwrapping another piece of their loot.

"Come to Poppa, you oh-so-chewable sugary confection," Bobby Bounder said, ignoring his brother's accusations.

"He's not going to listen," Bernie Bounder said, dragging a section of the candy pile closer to himself. "And neither is Balthasar."

Billy noticed that the monkey demon named Balthasar wasn't even unwrapping the treats; he was just shoving them into his gaping mouth, wrappers and all.

Disgusting.

One of the monkey demons suddenly began to shriek, leaping onto the makeshift table and bouncing up and down on a pair of metal-coiled shoes. Billy leaned over the edge of the catwalk a little farther so he could read the upset demon monkey's name.

This one was Bailey, and he didn't seem the least bit happy with his brothers.

"This bickering stops at once!" Bailey screamed, eyeing the four startled Rot-toothed Hopping Monkey Demons. They were all shocked into silence by the explosive outburst; even Balthasar had stopped shoving candy into his mouth.

"We're the Bounder boys," Bailey said, bouncing in

a slow, deliberate circle so that he could make eye contact with each of them. "Not the *Bicker* boys."

Balthasar thought that was pretty funny and began laughing uproariously—and then started to choke on the enormous wad of gum and wrappers crammed inside his mouth.

The monkey brothers watched him sputter and cough, none of them coming to his aid. Finally, when it looked as though he might just be done in by the huge chunk of gum, it shot from his mouth, ricocheting off a nearby wall and hitting Benny in the back of the head.

All the demon monkeys except for Benny, who rubbed furiously where he'd been struck with the disgusting glob, went into hysterics.

"You did that on purpose!" Benny spat. "I'll crush you flat for that!"

Benny leaped to his feet, bouncing in place furiously.

"You can try!" Balthasar retorted, now also standing upright and ready to hop into action.

"This is gonna be good," Bobby said, then greedily began grabbing more pieces of candy and shoving them into the pockets of his vest.

Bernie smacked the wrapped candies from his gluttonous brother's hands. "I'm sick of your greed," he snarled, baring jagged, yellow-stained teeth. "You'll not have another delectable morsel."

It looked as if Bernie and Bobby were going to go at it next while Bailey again tried to calm them all, hopping up and down and trying to be heard over their screeching monkey voices.

"One big happy family," Archebold said disgustedly.

"They seem a little high-strung," Billy observed. "Maybe they're eating too much sugar."

"You think?"

The Bounders were all up on their springs now, yelling at one another, jumping in place on their powerful spring shoes, ready to start a Slovakian Rot-toothed Hopping Monkey Demon rumble.

"Things are in chaos," Archebold suddenly said. "Now might be the time to make our move."

Billy scrambled eagerly to his feet. "All right," he said. "How should we do this?"

Archebold reached into his pocket. "First, we've got to let them know we're here, and who they're dealing with."

He pulled out what looked like a flashlight.

"I've been waiting to give this to you," he said, handing the light to Billy.

"But I've already got a flashlight," Billy said, unsnapping one of the pockets on his belt and removing a much smaller light. "See?"

Archebold laughed softly. "This is more than a mere

flashlight," he said, showing Billy a dark shape that was painted on the glass lens. "When we shine this down on them, the Owlboy symbol will be illuminated, and I'm betting they'll be so scared that they'll give up without a fight."

"You think?" Billy asked.

"Trust me," Archebold said, handing Billy the light. "Get ready to jump down there and accept their unconditional surrender."

Billy looked at the black symbol painted on the lens of the flashlight, trying to figure out exactly what it was supposed to be. He turned it around a few times, looking at it from different angles, before deciding that he should just trust the goblin and give it a try.

"Here goes," Billy said, standing up against the railing of the catwalk, clicking on the light and shining it down on one of the factory's dormant machines.

"Come at me, then," Balthasar Bounder was screaming, hopping from one foot to the other. "And when the blood and smoke have cleared, my wish to be an only child will have at last come true!"

"An only child with all the candy riches, right, Balthasar?" Benny asked, crouching down, ready to fight. "Isn't that what all this is about? You want it all for yourself?"

Bailey jumped between his brothers, sounding a little

bit like a talk-show host. "You see? This is what I'm talking about. How are we going to get anywhere in this cold cruel world if we can't learn to get along?"

"He started it," Benny retorted, pointing a long, clawed finger at Bobby.

"*I* started it?" Bobby questioned. "How dare you say—"

"Bobby may have started it, but I'm going to finish it!" Bernie screeched, throwing his spindly arms in the air, spittle flying from his mouth.

Balthasar dropped to his knees, eyes wild, eagerly grabbing up all the pieces of fallen candy and jamming them into his mouth as quickly as he could.

"I hate you," he was saying over and over again as his mouth became full and the words harder to understand. "I ate ugh ull!"

In all the drama, they still hadn't noticed the symbol shining on the machine behind them.

"They don't see it," Billy said to Archebold.

"Wiggle it a little," the goblin suggested.

"Like this?" Billy asked, moving the light beam around.

The monkey demons had all turned their anger on Balthasar, attempting to get their brother to spit out all the wrapped gum and candy he had shoveled into his mouth.

"He's eaten it all!" Benny wailed.

"Tainted! All of our delicious, sugary treasures have been tainted!" Bernie added.

Bobby pounced on his gluttonous brother, trying to pry his mouth open. "Grab his arms and legs. There's a chance we can still save some of it!"

Balthasar fought back fitfully as his brothers wrestled him to the floor.

It was Bailey Bounder who finally noticed, his attention suddenly drawn to the symbol dancing upon one of the factory's adhesive-storage tanks.

"Gotcha!" Archebold whispered excitedly, and Billy smiled. This was it! The chance to strike fear into the hearts of evildoers and let them know that Monstros had a new protector.

"What the heck is that?" Bailey asked, pointing to the black symbol within the circle of yellow that was illuminated upon the gray metal tank.

The Bounders stopped, releasing their brother. They all stared at the symbol.

"Looks like a moth," Benny said, tilting his head to one side to study the shape. "Yeah, that's a moth."

Bobby bounced a little closer to the tank. "That ain't a moth—that's a shark."

This wasn't going as expected. Billy glanced over at Archebold, whose face was buried in his hands as he shook his head in disgust.

"They're idiots," the goblin muttered. "Anyone with an ounce of brains could see what it is."

"Maybe we should just tell them what it is," Billy suggested.

"No," Archebold said firmly. "They'll figure it out eventually."

"How is that a shark?" Bernie asked. "Just looks like a black blot to me."

"No, it's a shark," Bobby said emphatically. "See . . . there's the dorsal fin."

Bailey Bounder had twisted himself in such a way that he was looking at it upside down. "If you look at it like this, it looks like some kind of pastry—perhaps an apple strudel."

With the mention of the sweet dessert, they all eagerly rubbed their hands together and licked their chops.

"What I wouldn't give for some apple strudel," Bobby said, wiping a thick dribble of spit from his chin.

"With a big mug of hot chocolate," Bernie contributed.

Growing impatient, Billy looked over at Archebold again. "I don't think these guys are ever going to figure this out," he announced.

Archebold nodded, and then his eyes suddenly got a wild look in them as he pointed back down to the factory floor. "Wait, this could be the break we're looking for."

Billy looked.

Balthasar was crawling across the floor, his eyes riveted to the illuminated spot.

"I know what it is," he said, wrapped pieces of spit-covered candy tumbling from his mouth as he spoke. "It's not a moth, or a shark, or even an apple strudel."

"What is it, brother?" Bernie asked.

Archebold reached out, slapping Billy on the arm. "Get ready. This is it."

Balthasar was practically on top of it, moving his head from side to side. "Yes, I do believe it to be so."

"Yes, Balthasar?" all the Bounders asked, anxiously awaiting their brother's observation.

"It's a chicken," he announced. "See?" The demon monkey pointed out some of the details to his brothers. "There's the little beak, there's the crest, and I think she's laying an egg."

Billy couldn't stand it anymore. He turned off the flashlight.

The Bounder boys gasped.

"Where'd the chicken go?" Denny asked.

"It's not a chicken, you dopes," Billy yelled down from the catwalk.

The Bounders all turned in the direction of his voice.

"It's an *owl* symbol," he said. "An *owl*—get it?"

He put his hands on his hips, making sure they got a good look at the costume.

The Bounders stared wide-eyed, their mouths agape. Billy was given a really good look at how disgusting their teeth were. *They really are Rot-toothed Hopping Monkey Demons*, he observed. *Those choppers have probably never seen a toothbrush or floss.*

"Wait a minute," Bailey Bounder said, rubbing his furry chin, obviously deep in thought. "Then you must be . . ."

"Chickenboy?" Balthasar suggested.

Bailey turned to slap the top of his brother's head. "It's an owl, not a chicken. Weren't you listening?"

Benny picked up where Bailey had left off. "If it's an owl, that would mean that you're . . ."

"Owlboy," they all said at the same time.

Billy stuck out his chest proudly. "Exactly," he said, striking a heroic pose.

"Excellent," Bailey said, a nasty smile forming on his horrible monkey face. "It's always good to know who you're about to destroy. It's much more personal that way."

And the monkey demons sprang into action.

"Get 'em, boys!"

It took everything Billy had and then some not to scream and run like a baby.

But he held his ground, Archebold bravely at his side, the fight scenes from all the Owlboy comics he had read over the last week playing in his head. The great hero of Monstros City always vanquished his enemies with an efficient combination of superior intelligence and strength.

Bailey Bounder was the first to land upon the catwalk.

"So, you're Owlboy, eh?" he asked with a nasty sneer. "A little short, don't you think?"

The other Bounders touched down behind their brother, one after the other, and slowly began to stalk toward them.

Billy and Archebold began to back away.

"So, what do you suggest?" Billy asked, not wanting to take his eyes from the advancing monkey demons.

"The usual, I guess," the goblin said. "Vanquish the villains, turn them in to the authorities, head back to the Roost for some congratulatory snacks."

"Sounds good, but here's the question," Billy said as the monkey demons came closer. "How do we vanquish the villains?"

"Hey, you're the one in the Owlboy costume," Archebold said. "I can't be expected to think of everything."

"Why did I know you were going to give me an answer like that?" Billy asked, deciding that he needed to do something, and fast.

But what?

He remembered a rope and grappling hook among the items Halifax had given him for his utility belt and thought those might be a good place to start. He quickly went through the pockets, still backing away from the stalking demons, until he found what he was looking for.

"Got any candy in them pouches?" Bobby Bounder asked as he wiped a trickle of spit from the corner of his mouth.

Ignoring him, Billy quickly pulled the long rope with the metal hook attached from inside the pouch on his belt, took aim and started to swing the rope around his head.

"Hold on," he said to Archebold as he let the line go, watching the weighted end sail through the air to hook onto a pipe that ran across the ceiling.

"I hope you know what you're doing," Archebold said, wrapping his tiny arms around Billy's waist.

"You and me both!" Billy added, leaping into the air.

Though terrified, Billy felt incredibly excited as he sailed through the air above the factory floor, unsure of what exactly was going to happen next.

"Where are we going?" Archebold asked, hanging on to Billy's waist for dear life.

"I haven't thought that far ahead yet," Billy answered, continuing to soar across the wide expanse. And then their swing came to an end, and they sailed back to the other side. "But I am open to suggestions."

The Bounders stood waiting on the catwalk, eagerly stretching out their long monkey arms, ready to catch Billy and Archebold as they swung back within reach.

"How about those boxes?" Archebold suggested, and Billy looked down to see a stack of cardboard boxes piled in a large recycling bin not too far below them.

They really didn't have much of a choice: either wind up in the clutches of the Bounder boys, dangle from the rope until Billy's arms got so tired that he couldn't hold on anymore, or swing over the boxes and try to make as soft a landing as possible. Billy glanced in the direction of the Bounders again and saw a grinning Bailey waiting, arms outstretched.

"Come to Poppa," the monkey demon snarled.

"In your dreams, creepazoid!" Billy yelled, thrusting out his legs to give them a bit more momentum.

And then he let go of the rope. He and Archebold fell toward the pile of boxes, hoping that they were filled with something soft, like pillows or maybe even packing peanuts. They hit the boxes and lay there for a moment, stunned by the impact but seemingly in one piece.

"You all right?" Billy asked Archebold as he scrambled to stand.

"Remind me again why I wanted to be Owlboy's sidekick so bad?" the goblin complained as Billy pulled him onto his feet.

"Didn't it have something to do with family tradition?"

"Possibly," Archebold said, brushing dirt from his coat. "But did I mention that insanity runs in my family? In fact, it gallops."

"Well, let's gallop out of here together before those Slovakian Rot-tooths crush us into pancakes."

Billy grabbed his goblin pal by the arm, pulling him across the factory floor.

The Bounders dropped down from the catwalk. The sound of the coils on their feet hitting the concrete floor made Billy and Archebold run faster.

"Don't run away, little Owlboy!" one of the Bounders called. "All we want to do is play with you."

"And then squash you flat," said another, and they all began to cackle maniacally.

"Maybe we *should've* started you off with something smaller," Archebold said as they ran through a doorway into a larger room filled with four big containers.

This must be where all the chemicals were mixed together to make the adhesive, Billy thought as he took in his surroundings. *The final product must have been stored inside those gigantic tanks.*

Billy heard the *sproing! sproing! sproing!* of the Bounder boots as the monkey demons chased after them. If he hadn't been running for his life, he would've been wicked bummed out. Not only was he letting Archebold down, he was letting the city of Monstros down as well.

Those old negative feelings were back with a vengeance, and Billy wondered why he'd ever believed he could actually be a super anything, never mind a hero.

Archebold was breathing pretty heavily and had started to slow down a bit. Figuring that the little guy could use a break—and that he himself could use a minute to gather his wits—Billy grabbed the goblin by his collar, yanking him down a dark passageway that ran between two of the huge storage tanks.

"I'm sorry about this, Archebold," Billy said as they hid in the shadows of the containers.

"Don't worry about it, kid," the goblin replied, dropping down to lean back against the storage tank. "I probably shouldn't have pushed you so hard . . . but you were doing so darn good."

Billy felt very inadequate standing there in his Owlboy suit. He was almost ashamed to be wearing it.

"Don't look so sad," Archebold said, attempting to cheer him up. "The Bounder boys are bad news. It was stupid of me to think even you could've stopped them."

And at that moment, Billy pretty much figured that his career as a superhero had come to a crashing end. He'd failed on his first real mission, and once word got out that the Bounders had kicked his costumed butt, he doubted that the citizens of Monstros would want anything to do with him as Owlboy.

"I guess I'm just not as good as you thought I was," Billy said, his confidence leaking away. He hung his head, feeling the most depressed he'd felt since his dad accidentally sprayed the garden hose over his issue of *The Snake: King-Size Summer Special Number One*.

But at least he'd been able to get a new copy of the ultrarare comic. This was an altogether different situation. Nobody could make him a hero; this was something he had to do himself.

And he had screwed it up big-time.

Archebold didn't say a word, only reinforcing how disappointed he must be.

Billy wanted to crawl underneath a rock and hide.

The Bounders were close, the bouncing of their coiled-spring shoes on the factory floor momentarily distracting Billy and Archebold from their disappointment.

"Come out, come out, wherever you are, puny

Owlboy," Bailey Bounder called as his brothers jeered in the background. "We'll try not to make your stomping hurt too bad."

Archebold looked at Billy, his goblin eyes wide and glistening in the shadows. "We'd better get you out of here before you get hurt," he said, and started to stand—but for some reason he couldn't.

"What the . . . ," the goblin sputtered. "Great! I think I'm stuck."

"Stuck to what?" Billy asked, unable to see much in the darkness around them.

Archebold continued to struggle as Billy pulled the tiny flashlight from his utility belt and shone it down upon the ground. The tank of adhesive was leaking, and Archebold was stuck to the puddle of glue that had collected on the floor.

"You're stuck, all right," Billy agreed. He shone his light on the tank, finding the riveted seam in the metal where the sticky stuff had seeped out. "The tank's leaking," he told his friend. "Give me your hand and I'll try to pull you free."

Billy put his light away and took the goblin's arms. "On a count of three. One . . . two . . . *three!*"

Prepared to use his Monstros City superstrength, Billy tugged with all his might, and Archebold came free with a loud ripping sound.

"What the . . . ?" Archebold said, looking over his shoulder. The butt of his tuxedo pants had been torn away, the material still stuck to the glue on the ground.

Billy was surprised to see that the goblin was wearing pink boxer shorts with great big red hearts on them. He would've bet good money on Archebold's being a tighty-whitey sort of guy.

"I'm really sorry, Archebold," Billy said. "I didn't think the glue was that sticky, and . . ."

Suddenly, it hit him with the force of a phaser on stun: an idea that could very well change everything.

"Hey, Billy," Archebold said to him. "What's wrong, kid? Snap out of it. They're only pants. I've got at least six pairs back at the Roost, no need to go into shock or anything."

"I have a plan," Billy said simply, a sly smile that he couldn't control creeping across his face. "I know how we can defeat the Bounders."

"You do?" Archebold asked, self-consciously covering his exposed rear end with his hands.

Billy nodded, seeing the master plan unfold inside his head.

"I'm gonna need a big bucket."

*　*　*

Billy watched as Archebold strolled out into the middle of the factory floor, whistling a casual tune as if he didn't have a care in the world—other than the fact that he had a pack of Slovakian Rot-toothed Hopping Monkey Demons after him—and that he wasn't wearing any pants.

They'd found a bucket in a janitor's closet not too far from where they had been resting, and Billy had immediately put his plan into motion.

The Bounders were somewhere inside the large room, probably lying in wait for Billy and the goblin. Billy hated to hold the poor guys up any longer than he had to.

"Yoo-hoo, Bounder boys!" Archebold called in a high-pitched voice that made him sound like Billy's aunt Mildred. "Here I am, all alone and helpless."

Billy stuck his head around the corner to see if the monkey demons would take the bait.

His plan involved glue from the storage tank. Using his enhanced strength, he had managed to pull at the already loose seam of the tank, making the leak even bigger. He then filled the bucket they had found with the supersticky substance.

Archebold was doing some kind of crazy dance now, wiggling his butt in its heart-printed underwear in all directions as he attempted to draw the Bounders out from hiding. He was the perfect lure; how could anybody—especially a Slovakian Rot-toothed Hopping Monkey Demon wearing bounding boots—not want to crush him into paste?

"C'mon, boys," Archebold called. "I'm getting kind of bored here. I thought you guys were supposed to be scary. Yeah, you're scary, all right. You're so scary I'm about to take my behind out of here and head on home to bed, that's how scary you are."

The goblin looked over at Billy and shrugged. "I don't know where they are," he whispered. "Maybe they suspect it's a trap."

"You've got to get them really mad," Billy suggested. "Maybe say something nasty about their teeth . . . or even better, their mother."

As far as Billy was concerned, there was nothing worse than insulting somebody's mother, and he guessed the creatures would likely have the same feeling here in Monstros City.

"Breaking out the heavy artillery, eh?" Archebold commented. "I like the way you think, boss. I've got just the right thing. Heard a heckleberry pie say this once, and I've been saving it up for a special occasion."

The goblin turned his attention back to the broad expanse of the room, his eyes darting around, searching for any signs of the nasty monkeys. They remained hidden.

"Hey, Bounders," Archebold called. "Got a question for you guys. Is it true that your mother was so fat that she donated a hundred pounds to charity?"

Billy gasped from his hiding place. *Good one, Archebold,* he thought. That one would have surely sent any sixth grader at Connery Elementary School into fits of rage.

But the goblin wasn't stopping there.

"Or how about the recent rumors that your mom's so dumb that when stopped for breaking the speed limit, she offered to try to fix it?"

Billy winced. A double play: a *Your mom's so fat* followed by a *Your mom's so dumb*. He imagined that hurt big-time.

And he was right.

Screams of anger echoed around the abandoned factory, and Billy peered around the corner again to see the Bounders emerge from hiding. They were bouncing crazily across the factory floor, making their way toward a seemingly frozen Archebold.

"How dare you speak about our beloved mother in such a way!" Bailey cried.

"She thought she was doing something to help the community when she gave up that fat!" Bobby bellowed.

"And that business with the traffic cop was all a horrible misunderstanding," Balthasar assured them. "Not that you care, you heartless, craven monster!"

Billy was actually a little surprised at how upset they seemed. It just went to show how dangerous it could be to make fun of somebody's mother, even the mother of a pack of Slovakian Rot-toothed Hopping Monkey Demons.

"What should I do?" Archebold asked, eyes riveted on the demons bouncing toward him.

"Stay right there," Billy said. "Don't move an inch."

"Great," the goblin scoffed. "It was nice knowing you, kid. Hope you enjoy having Halifax as your new sidekick."

Billy ignored him, watching as the Bounders bounded toward their prey.

Any second now, he thought, readying his bucket.

Billy waited until he could read their nametags. At the last possible second, he jumped out and splashed the sticky contents of the bucket onto the floor in front of Archebold.

The Bounders roared when they saw Billy, not paying the least attention to the spot where the coils on their Bounder boots were about to land.

Holding his breath, Billy crossed his fingers, toes and eyes, hoping that his plan would work. If it failed, both he and Archebold were in some serious trouble.

The coils landed in the goopy substance congealing on the floor and stuck fast. The thick metal springs stretched upward but stayed stuck to the floor. One by one, the Bounders were caught in the glue trap.

"What's going on?" Bailey said, trying desperately to pull his boots from the muck.

"It's glue, I think," Bobby answered, his voice filling with panic. "We're stuck!"

"This can't be happening!" Benny wailed, tugging on his ankles, trying to pull his feet out of the special boots.

Balthasar was way ahead of them and was actually managing to untie his boots and remove his feet, only to fall flat on his face and become stuck to the floor in the slowly expanding puddle of glue.

"A little help here!" he cried. But his brothers ignored his pleas, more concerned with their own predicament.

"That was some plan you had," Archebold said, cheerfully giving Billy a high five. "Only a real successor to the Owlboy mantle could come up with something like that, let me tell you."

Billy felt his mood soar higher than ever before. He'd been so bummed mere minutes ago that he hadn't thought he could ever feel this good again. "It was nothing," he said modestly. "Just needed a minute or so to put on my thinking cap and then it just sort of came to me."

Bailey Bounder let out a ferocious shriek that made the hair on the back of Billy's neck stand at attention.

"When I get out of here, I'll make you wish you'd never heard the name Owlboy," he snarled ferociously.

Billy was about to come back with something clever like *Oh yeah* or *You and whose army* when there was an even louder commotion and the Monstros City police force made its grand entrance.

"Put your paws, tentacles, feelers, claws or whatever you got in the air, you're all under arrest!" Chief Bloodwart hollered, striding into the storage area with his men.

Detective Oozea was slithering around the Bounders, making sure to stay clear of the sticky puddle of glue.

"They got us stuck," he heard one of the Bounder boys complain to the gelatinous detective.

"And they made fun of our mother," proclaimed another.

Oozea rubbed his rubbery chin with a stubby tentacle. "Is it true that she got pulled over for breaking the speed limit and then offered to fix it?"

The detective and some of the other uniformed officers started laughing as the Bounders crossed their arms, stewing.

Archebold tugged Billy's arm. "Quick, let's get out of here or we'll be here all night answering their questions."

Billy allowed himself to be pulled toward the back of the factory, but not before making eye contact with the rocky-skinned police chief.

The chief began to speak, and Billy was certain that he was about to order them to come back.

But he was wrong.

"Good job, Owlboy!" Chief Bloodwart called.

And at that very moment, Billy Hooten truly believed that he was a hero named Owlboy.

Wasn't that the craziest thing?

CHAPTER 12

Billy stood at the wall of Owlboy portraits in the snack room, drinking his mug of ghost juice—a thick but invisible liquid made from the fruit of the bogey bush, which, according to Archebold, who loved the stuff, ripened only once a year in the spectral fields of the Phantom Farms. Billy was wondering if someday there would be a picture of him hanging on the wall.

"So what do you think?" Billy asked his friend, who was sitting across the room in an overstuffed chair, eating from a bowl that was filled to overflowing with what looked like tiny multicolored brains.

Billy took up a position in an empty space large enough for another portrait and posed, holding his mug of ghost juice. "Will I fit in with the others?" he asked Archebold.

"You'll fit just fine," the goblin answered, popping a handful of colorful brains into his mouth and starting to chew.

Billy returned to his own comfortable chair. "Bet you wouldn't have thought that before I came up with that plan to stop the Bounder boys," he challenged, helping himself to a piece of fluffy white cake so light it floated above the plate like a cloud.

Archebold set the bowl of brains down, licked his clawed fingers and wiped his hands on the front of his new pants. As soon as they had returned to the Roost, he had immediately gone to his room for a fresh pair, complaining all the while that his legs were cold.

"I did have my doubts for a bit there," the goblin admitted. "But much to my pleasure, you proved me wrong."

Billy finished his piece of cloud cake, enjoying the strangely pleasant sensation of the dessert floating around inside his stomach. "*You* had doubts!" he exclaimed. "I was ready to take off the costume right then and there—but then I would have been practically naked, too—so I guess I had to come up with something else."

"And there was only room for one of us to be nearly

naked on this case," Archebold said with a wink, and laughed.

"Better you than me," Billy said, starting to giggle.

The goblin took the pitcher of ghost juice from the table. "Give me your mug," he said, and Billy held it out for the goblin to refill.

Well, at least he thought it was filled, but how could he tell—the drink was invisible.

Archebold refilled his own glass, then held it up.

"I want to propose a toast."

Billy lifted his mug.

"To Billy Hooten, the newest Owlboy," Archebold proclaimed, his dark, beady eyes twinkling proudly. "Evil doesn't stand a chance."

Two pitchers of ghost juice and more snacks than either of them could keep count of later, Billy and Archebold sat in their comfy chairs, stuffed close to bursting.

"I think if I ate another bite I might explode," Billy said, patting his swollen belly with a gloved hand.

"I can just imagine how mad Halifax would be, having to scrub burst superhero off the walls," Archebold said, leaning over to help himself to a giant chocolate-covered slug.

Billy felt his eyes growing heavy. He knew he would

soon lose the battle against sleep. "I think I should probably be heading home," he said, stifling a yawn.

"I'm pretty tired myself," the goblin agreed, sliding off his chair. "C'mon, I'll show you the way out."

Billy followed his tiny friend through the winding hallways of the Roost, struggling to keep his eyes open and wondering if this was how it felt to sleepwalk. The two at last ended up in the observation room, the hundreds of television screens still tuned to the various locations and happenings in the city of monsters.

Something caught Billy's eye, and he strolled closer to one of the monitors. "What's that?" he asked, thinking there might be a situation brewing that could require his attention.

But it wasn't trouble at all. Quite the opposite, really. There was a party going on in the streets. All kinds of monsters were dancing and laughing and having a general good time.

"What's going on?" Archebold asked, rubbing sleep from his eyes as he trudged over to stand beside Billy. "Well, I'll be. Would you look at that," he continued, his voice filled with awe.

And then Billy noticed the signs.

WELCOME BACK, OWLBOY! read one of them.

WE MISSED YOU! read another.

"It's really something, isn't it?" Archebold said, putting a friendly arm around Billy's waist.

"Yeah, it really is," Billy agreed, pulling his tired eyes from the scene playing out on the television and walking with the goblin to the door that would lead him back to the shadowy passage, and finally to the stairs, and home.

"See you soon?" Archebold asked, opening the door for him.

Billy stopped, turning to his new friend.

"What do you think?"

Night-vision goggles activated, Billy walked through the dark, twisting passage until he reached the stairs that would take him back up into the normal world.

Billy didn't think he'd ever quite reach the end as he trudged up the curving stone staircase, but he got a second wind when he saw a light growing gradually closer above. He was truly exhausted, his first real adventure as Monstros' superhero rattling around inside his skull as he at last crawled out of the stone Sprylock coffin.

Billy thought it was sort of weird; as he looked around the dusty old mausoleum, it felt good to be back in the real world, but at the same time he found himself missing the bizarre sights of Monstros City.

He left the mausoleum as he had found it, closing the door behind him and jogging down the cemetery path toward the wall that separated his yard from the final resting place of the dead.

Billy wasn't sure he had ever been so tired. He remembered a time when he and Tommy Stanley had stayed up all night watching horror movies, eating frozen pizzas and reading comic books. This time, he was even tireder than that.

Over the wall and then into the house, he thought, trying to psych himself up. The image of his nice, comfortable bed was the most wonderful vision he had ever seen, and he yearned to crawl beneath the cool sheets, blanket and heavy comforter.

Hopping up onto the wall, minus his superabilities, and dropping down into his yard, he reminded himself to be extra quiet. He wouldn't want to wake his parents and have to explain why he was dressed the way he was.

As he crossed the yard, he glanced across the way to Victoria's house. Remembering his promise to play superhero with her the next day if she went to bed, he half expected to see her tiny face appear suddenly in the window.

That should be fun, he thought sarcastically, climbing the porch steps and letting himself in, but he was too tired to worry about it now. He'd deal with it in the morning, after he'd had a chance to rest.

Billy stood in the kitchen, carefully listening, and

heard the sounds of gunfire and explosions coming from the television in the other room. The movie his folks had been watching—sleeping through was more like it—was still playing, and he again marveled at how different the passage of time was in this world and in Monstros. According to the kitchen clock, he'd been gone for less than forty minutes.

It was an amazing thing.

Creeping down the hallway, he peered into the living room to see his folks still fast asleep in front of the TV.

Perfect, Billy thought, beginning the last leg of his journey up the stairs and to bed. But the closer he got to his room, the more his experiences bubbled up in his thoughts, and the more excited he became.

He couldn't wait to do it all again, but first he needed to sleep. Too tired even to wash his face and brush his teeth, he removed his Owlboy costume, taking the time to put it on a hanger—which might have been a first for any article of clothing he had ever owned. He held the costume out at arm's length, admiring it and what it represented before hanging it far back in the closet.

His bed seemed to call to him, speaking in the language of sleep, and Billy answered its siren call, shuffling zombie-like across the room and falling onto his mattress. He barely had the strength to cover himself before drifting off into a deep, dreamless sleep.

Billy Hooten didn't need to dream. His dreams had become reality.

Archebold the goblin reclined in the observation room chair, watching the many television monitors.

One in particular.

He heard the door open, heard the shuffling footfalls that could only be Halifax coming up to stand alongside him.

"Hello," the troll said. He was holding a broom and started to sweep the floor. "Mind if I tidy up a bit in here?" he asked.

"Knock yourself out," Archebold said, eyes fixed on the monitor.

The troll swept for a while, humming softly beneath his breath.

"So how did it go tonight?" he asked casually, sweeping some dust bunnies—which actually looked like tiny rabbits—into a small pile.

"Went good," the goblin answered. "Thanks for that information tonight, by the way. It really helped out. Sorry we got you out of your bath."

"No problem. I needed to get out anyway, my fingers

were getting all pruny." The troll wiggled his sausage-sized fingers.

"I hate when that happens," Archebold added, eyes still fixed on the monitor.

"So, this new kid," Halifax asked, leaning on his broom. "Think he's going to work out?"

Archebold said nothing, reaching down between the cushions of the recliner for the remote control. Programming a code on the remote, he pointed it at the monitors and pushed a button.

All the monitors flickered momentarily before returning to normal, but they no longer showed multiple views of what was going on in Monstros City. Now they showed only one scene, a scene of celebration.

A celebration of Owlboy's return.

Archebold turned his head to look at Halifax, who was staring at the images, surprise showing on his hairy face.

"Do I think the kid's going to work out?" the goblin asked with a sly smile.

"What do *you* think?"

EPILOGUE

The weekend had gone by way too fast, but didn't they all?

Billy sat at his usual table in the cafeteria late on Monday morning with the regular cast of characters, biting his tongue to keep from spilling the beans about his weekend adventures.

Danny was talking about his mold collection to no one in particular, while Dwight regaled Reggie with tales of a sleepover he'd gone to at his cousin's house, where they were allowed to watch an R-rated movie and stay up as late as they wanted. Kathy B was reading Shakespeare's *Macbeth* out loud, doing all the parts with different, wacky accents.

A typical Monday lunchtime at Connery Elementary School.

But Billy's weekend had been far from typical. Since Friday night he had gone back to Monstros City twice. He would have visited more if not for his weekend chores and having to play superhero with Victoria on Saturday morning. Each visit to Monstros had been more incredible than the last, and he couldn't wait to go back.

"What did you do this weekend, Billy?" Danny asked before taking an enormous bite of a very red Delicious apple.

Kathy B looked up from *Macbeth*. "Did thou doest anything fun?" she asked in a booming voice, as if she were performing onstage.

Reggie picked at something caught in the elaborate wirework of his braces, waiting for Billy's reply.

"Bet you didn't see an R-rated movie or stay up as late as I did," Dwight challenged.

Incredible images of what he had experienced— what he had done—flooded Billy's mind, adventures that even he wouldn't have believed if somebody had told him about them.

Which was why he would keep his mouth shut. This was his special secret; it belonged to him alone.

"Nope, I didn't," Billy answered Dwight. "Just a

typical weekend." He took a big bite of his sandwich to keep from laughing insanely as he thought of being chased by the Bounder boys and driving through the streets of Monstros City in the coolest car that had ever existed. "Really kind of boring."

As they finished up their lunches, they all agreed on how boring the weekends could sometimes be.

Billy stuffed his trash inside his lunch bag and was just getting up to throw it away when he heard a familiar voice call out from across the lunchroom.

"Hey, guys," Randy Kulkowski hollered, loudly enough for the entire lunchroom to hear. "There goes Billy Hooten . . . Owlboy."

Randy's cronies all started to laugh.

But Billy didn't mind. For the first time he could remember, Randy Kulkowski was right.

He *was* Owlboy.

THOMAS E. SNIEGOSKI is a novelist and comic book scripter who has worked for every major company in the comics industry.

As a comic book writer, his work includes *Stupid, Stupid Rat Tails*, a miniseries prequel to the international hit *Bone*. He has also written tales featuring such characters as Hellboy, Batman, Daredevil, Wolverine, and the Punisher.

He is also the author of the groundbreaking quartet of teen fantasy novels entitled The Fallen, the first of which (*Fallen*) has just been produced as a television movie for the ABC Family Channel. The two books in his Sleeper Conspiracy, a new series, *Sleeper Code* and *Sleeper Agenda*, have just been released. With Christopher Golden, he is the coauthor of the dark fantasy series The Menagerie, as well as the young readers' fantasy series OutCast, recently optioned by Universal Pictures. Sniegoski and Golden also wrote the graphic novel *BPRD: Hollow Earth*, a spinoff of the fan favorite comic book series Hellboy.

Sniegoski was born and raised in Massachusetts, where he still lives with his wife, LeeAnne, and their Labrador retriever, Mulder. Please visit the author at www.sniegoski.com.

ERIC POWELL is the writer and artist of the award-winning comic book series The Goon for Dark Horse Comics. He has also contributed work to such comic titles as *Arkham Asylum*, *Buffy the Vampire Slayer*, *Hellboy: Weird Tales*, *Star Wars Tales*, *The Incredible Hulk*, *MAD Magazine*, *Swamp Thing*, and *The Simpsons*.